Wanted by the Marshal

Wanted by the Marshal

An Angel Point Romance

Susan Lute

TULE
PUBLISHING

Chapter One

S HE WAS DRIVING a long way from her mostly comfortable attic apartment in San Francisco in order to talk her baby sister out of making the biggest mistake of her life. At least U.S. Marshal Dakota James hoped that's what she was doing. The only hiccup in her plan was Taylor. The kid knew her own mind and wouldn't hesitate to tell big sister it was presumptuous to believe she'd suddenly lost it because she was marrying a near stranger.

What other option did Dakota have? Stand by and do nothing? She couldn't do it.

The drive north from San Francisco under clear skies, windows down to let in the salt-scented air as the road periodically took Dakota close to the ocean, was calming. What did they call it in those self-help books? A Zen experience.

It wasn't exactly that, but it was close enough and a nice change from the pressure of work that had gotten her put on leave in the middle of a major drug case.

Just north of Gold Beach, Oregon, she spotted a pickup parked on the side of the road. The right-side rear hung from a jack. An older gentleman, with white hair looking like it hadn't seen a comb in recent days, struggled with the tire. He was dressed in jeans and a plaid shirt with sleeves rolled up to his elbows. Back rounded at the shoulders, he didn't appear to be a day under eighty.

Feeling an absurd kind of kinship with the broken-down vehicle, Dakota pulled up behind the older Chevy. Getting cautiously out of her Mustang, she approached the man with caution. You could never be too careful. Trouble, in her experience anyway, could come in the most benign-looking packages.

"Need some help?"

Straightening his back, the older gent pushed a hand through his hair, making the disorderly waves worse. "Not many girls know how to change a tire."

"I can do it. Been taking care of my own tires for a long time." She couldn't help the wink and smile she sent his way. He was cute in an engaging, octogenarian way.

"What's your name, young lady?"

"Dakota James, sir."

He glanced at her Mustang. Bushy eyebrows arched, but he didn't comment. She knew what he saw. A Marine medallion on the back window proclaimed, at least until recently, she'd spent a good share of her adult working life in the Marine Corps. The medallion had been there since the day she finished the car's restoration.

"Claude Henley. Let's see what you've got."

Even with him hovering over her shoulder, it didn't take Dakota long to get the tire changed. When she was done, she put his tools in the toolbox in the back of the truck. "That should do it. You're all set to go."

"Hold on a second. I've got something for you. A small thank you for helping a stranded old man."

"No thanks necessary. I'm happy to help," she said, backing toward the Mustang.

"Wait."

From ingrained habit, the firm command stopped her where she was.

Claude reached into the cab of the truck. He came back carrying what looked like an old-fashioned metal lunchbox. When he flipped opened the lid, on one side was a thermos, on the other a sandwich and cookies in separate baggies. He held out the bag of cookies. "My wife baked these."

Dakota put up a hand to stop him. "Really. You don't have to give me anything. You needed help. I just happened to be the lucky one passing by."

He gently took her hand and, wrapping her fingers around the package of cookies, looked her squarely in the eyes. "I insist. These cookies are made from a recipe that's been passed down in my wife's family for generations. I only share them with special people."

"But—" *I'm not special.*

"No arguments now." He was a stubborn old cuss. "To quote George Eliot in *Middlemarch*, 'people glorify all sorts of bravery, except the bravery they might show on behalf of their nearest neighbor.'" He squeezed her hand. "Thank you."

Abruptly, he let her go, climbed into his truck and with a jaunty wave, drove off. Dakota stood there for a long moment, alternating staring at the cookies and watching him drive away.

She blinked, climbed behind the wheel of her car and, digging one of the cookies out of the baggy, took a bite. She closed her eyes in appreciation.

When was the last time anyone had called her special? Or brave? Lifting her chin, she followed Claude's example. No more wasting time. She had someplace to be and a mission to complete.

When she reached the outskirts of Angel Point, the Oregon coastal town looked a little windblown, but not nearly as frayed around the edges as Dakota felt. She parked the Mustang close to The Chowder House. The 1966 red Ford was her baby. The only one she was ever likely to have. She'd gotten the little beast, a classic—and more dependable than anything else in her life had been for a very long time—for a song and had it restored to its original condition. Her efforts on her own behalf hadn't been as successful.

After showing her identification, the front desk gal at the sheriff's department told Dakota she could find Taylor having lunch with her fiancé at The Chowder House. Apparently, the restaurant was best known for its clam chowder. That's what the sign out front said.

Inside, she found her sister talking to her guy at a table on the far side of the room, close against a bank of windows overlooking lush landscape. Her sister's back was to the room, an odd thing for a James to do. *How could you see trouble coming if you weren't watching for it?*

Dakota pressed her lips into a straight line. Adams didn't appear to be a man in love. A man in love didn't look bored, his entire attention focused on his phone instead of his lunch date.

He finally leaned back in his chair, with one jean-covered leg stretched out, foot encased in a well-worn cowboy boot. He finished a text before laying his cell on the table and responding to something Taylor said.

"Come to Angel Point to celebrate my engagement to the love of my life," Taylor had insisted the last time they talked.

Love? Dakota wasn't really a believer.

And Adams proved it. There was no light of that illusive phenomenon on his face when he gazed at Taylor. Okay, he was handsome. It appeared he had good taste in boots. She would give Taylor that, but there was no spark in his body language that said she was his one and only. He didn't lean toward his fiancé as if every minute she wasn't in his arms was torture.

Dakota didn't know what love was supposed to look like, except she was pretty sure what she was looking at wasn't it.

Not that long ago, New Year's Day in fact—the one day every year when she and Taylor made it a point to get together—they'd enjoyed a good laugh over neither of the James sisters having a date for New Year's Eve, because getting a date to stay past the appetizers was nearly impossible. It said something that today the plate of appetizers between Adams and her sister looked like it hadn't been touched. Her Spidey sense was right. There definitely was a problem.

Why had the kid agreed to marry Adams? The man looked more like a construction worker than a doctor. Not that there was anything wrong with a good-looking, hunky construction worker. Taylor just didn't usually go for the cowboy type who built things with his hands and came home wearing the results of his day on his clothes.

A part of Dakota wished she believed in love with the same gusto Taylor did. And that she could be happy for her sister. Perhaps then she might be persuaded to date someone with Adams's strong shoulders and broad chest.

She took a step toward Taylor. Having this conversation over the phone would have saved her a lot of time and miles of wear and tear on her Mustang. Unfortunately for the forced leave she'd thought to turn into a vacation on Oahu, this was a mission that needed to be conducted face-to-face.

She squared her shoulders. A skirmish with Taylor, no matter how serious, was always fun.

"Can I show you to a table?" The woman asking had

thick, auburn hair that fell in waves to her shoulders and a smile in her light brown eyes.

"No, thank you." She gestured vaguely in Taylor's direction. "My party's just over there."

"Okay, then. Your server will be right with you." The woman turned to the next person behind Dakota. A line had formed while she'd been scoping out the terrain.

As she wove between tables, Adams's gaze shifted. His brows lifted when he saw her. Her stomach took a tumble as he pulled his booted foot under his chair and angled forward on his elbows.

The closer she got, the better she could see the flicker of male interest growing in a gaze that drifted slowly over the loose white, button-down shirt tucked into the jeans she wore instead of her usual marshal's getup.

Irritation—definitely irritation, not attraction—took her by surprise. A flirty grin spread across his handsome face. Before she could put a kibosh on her runaway thoughts, Dakota actually thought *cute . . . on the market? Yum!*

OMG! What was she doing? And was the dude actually sending *I like you, let's play* vibes to his fiancé's sister? He definitely didn't have that bored look on his face any longer.

Her heart skipping more than a beat or two, she gave herself a mental hand slap and crossed the intervening space, only stopping her outraged march once she reached Taylor's elbow. Sisters did not poach each other's guy!

She sent Adams a glare that in her drill sergeant days had

made raw recruits shiver in their new combat boots. After silently promising she'd never think of him as a hunky, sexy guy again, she opened her mouth to extricate her sister from this . . . this . . . playboy's clutches.

Before the words tumbled out, Taylor realized she was there and jumped out of her chair. "Kodie! You made it." Slender arms wrapped around Dakota's neck. "I'm so glad you're here."

Only Taylor had the power to cheer her up when her life was at its worst. Closing her eyes, almost able to ignore the rush from Adams's unexpected flirting, Dakota savored the hug and squeezed her sister back.

Still, she had to tell Taylor her guy was a player. Pulling back from her sister's embrace, Dakota forced the words past the guilty lump in her throat. "Listen—"

Adams had risen from his chair, his expression carefully blank now. Served him right that he was totally getting outed.

"When did you get into town?" Indicating an empty chair at the table, Taylor gave a tug on her hand.

"About twenty minutes ago. Look, Taylor, I need to talk to you."

Her sister waved a hand at Adams. "This is—"

"You can't marry this . . . this guy," Dakota blurted.

"Beckett Leland," Taylor said at the same time.

"I certainly hope not," a male voice behind Dakota joined in. "Especially since she's already engaged to me and it's against the law for a lady to be married to two guys at the same time. A sheriff should know better."

Dakota spun around, coming face-to-face with a tall, better-than-average-looking man, who was trying very hard to smother his laughter.

If she weren't so embarrassed at her gaffe, she might laugh too. But another mistake in a long line of mistakes just wasn't funny.

He held out his hand. "I'm the real Dr. Gabe Adams. You must be Taylor's sister, Kodie."

"Dakota," she said, clenching her jaw.

Taylor was the only one who got to call her Kodie, the nickname Frank had given her when she was a little girl, when the sun still rose and set on the man she'd once called "Dad."

A flush climbed up her neck to burn her cheeks. Straightening, she took the hand the real Adams offered.

"Nice to meet you." When she made an error, Dakota owned up to it. Refusing to look at the guy she'd mistaken for her sister's fiancé—he was probably having a good laugh—she cleared her throat. "Sorry about the mix-up. I didn't mean to . . ."

"No worries." Adams's reassurance didn't bank the twitch at the corners of his mouth or the amusement flooding his astute gaze.

Placing a conciliatory hand on her shoulder, he leaned around her to kiss Taylor. "Did you get yourself engaged to this scruffy Marine while I was seeing patients this morning?"

Taylor laughed. "No. Just a case of mistaken identity. Besides, Beckett's not my type."

Let the scruffy Marine laugh. Dakota had been in more mortifying situations. Like when Granger had given her the boot right in the middle of an important case hunting down drug runners on the West Coast, and then ordered her not to come back to work for two weeks. All because her concentration was shot to heck.

Unfortunately, she'd been unable to turn that particular lemon into lemonade and had made a rookie mistake. A decorated Marine turned Marshals Special Operations should have gathered more intel before beginning a mission. Even if that mission was a civilian one. No wonder Granger had put her on leave.

There must be a way out that didn't involve taking another hike across the crowded restaurant. Her gaze latched onto a canine tail on the other side of Leland. The dog lay with his head on his paws, dark eyes on her face. The animal wore a red service vest. Had Leland been injured in some way that wasn't obvious? There was no time to find out. Still, seeing the dog here was . . . soothing.

"I've got to go."

"But you just got here," Taylor protested.

Three pairs of eyes watched her. Four, if she counted the dog. Taylor looked confused. Dakota didn't blame her.

There was something disconcerting about emotions that wouldn't go back in the box where they belonged.

Adams pulled out a chair. "Stay. Please. Have lunch with us. Or, if you want, Beckett and I can take off, so you girls can catch up."

"You don't have to leave." Reluctantly sinking into the chair Adams offered, Dakota leaned uncomfortably on her elbows.

She focused on the sound of conversations from the other diners—which wasn't as easy as it should have been, the smell of food as plates passed by the table, while making a mental list of small details around the room. The soft green of the walls. Mismatched chairs strategically placed around the tables. White, lace-patterned tablecloths.

Blinking rapidly, she pushed back on the emotions from the past that had started erupting like one of Yellowstone's geysers after that last emergency response at Marine base in South Carolina.

Adams hovered beside her chair. Taylor clung tightly to her hand.

"I'm okay," Dakota reassured them on a deep breath, half laughing at her partial success. "Nothing to see here. Honest."

A booted foot nudged hers under the table. She turned to Leland and found blueberries. His eyes were the color of blueberries. And she owed him big time for the distraction.

"What's your dog's name?"

"Tucker." He scratched the dog's head. Only the shepherd's deep brown eyes shifted in his owner's direction.

Adams took a seat on the other side of the square table. Dakota was grateful. The last thing she needed was for Taylor to discover her in-control big sister had let the genie out of the bottle and couldn't put him back in. She'd caused enough of a stir already.

A waitress came to take their order. Though she wasn't really hungry, Dakota ordered the first thing she saw on the menu. And coffee. She needed lots of coffee.

As the others placed their orders, she twisted her fingers into knots in her lap. For crying out loud. A James who couldn't lock down her feelings? How humiliating was that?

Dakota pasted a smile on her face, hoping it looked real. She'd come to Angel Point to convince Taylor to protect her heart. That conversation would have to come later. Now was no longer the time nor place.

The tension racing through her veins eased off. She broke into the uneasy silence, asking, "Can anyone recommend a good hotel?"

"You can stay with me," Taylor and Adams said at the same time.

Adams took Taylor's hand. "Frank is staying with you."

Dakota watched, a little fascinated, as Taylor let Adams anchor her by the simple touch. Her sister was as independent and self-reliant as they came. The smile the two shared, the stars in their eyes—as if they were in the restaurant all by themselves—shook Dakota's firm belief that love wouldn't last. In her thirty-one years, she'd certainly found no evidence that it could. The tender moment didn't change her mind on that score.

It took a moment, but Adams's words finally filtered through her brain fog. "Frank's in town?"

Great. Running into Frank was not part of her plan.

"He's been staying in my spare room, but he's not here right now. He's in San Antonio, selling his house."

"Why is he selling his house?"

Taylor countered. "When was the last time you talked to him?"

"It's been a while," Dakota admitted stiffly. The last time, she'd been trying to forget and was just this side of sloppy drunk. Of course, the alcohol hadn't fixed anything. She should have known better.

"I know he wants to be the one to tell you." Taylor put her napkin aside, turning so she faced Dakota squarely. "I thought he called."

"He may have." She had no appetite for telling her sister, in the middle of a crowded restaurant, that she'd blocked his calls because . . . well, just because.

Her relationship with Frank had been a rocky road from the minute she'd lost her perfect family on the day her mother left. When he came to visit and found Dakota alone, drowning herself in whatever liquor she could lay her hands on, and thinking he could tell her how to fix her life when he had no clue how to fix his own—

That had been the final straw. It was easy after that to hit block on his phone number.

"He's retiring." Taylor took a deep breath. "And getting married."

"Married?" She managed to keep her voice as reasonable as possible. Who would want to marry Frank? His track record was the worst.

Dakota would never forget hiding in the bathroom, covering her ears during Frank and Laney's bitter fights at the end, before her mother finally packed her bags, leaving them all behind. Frank and Laney were poster children for love imploding long before getting to their unlikely happy-ever-after. And her family . . . well, they'd never been the same since.

"And he's retiring? Workaholic Deputy Marshal Frank James? Are we talking about the same guy?"

Grinning, Taylor nodded. Dakota hadn't seen that spontaneous sweet smile since they were little girls.

"Shocking, I know. I didn't believe it at first, either."

An unfamiliar longing seeped through Dakota as she wondered—not for the first time—what their lives would look like now if things had turned out differently between Frank and Laney.

"Who's the unlucky lady?" she asked, taking a healthy gulp of coffee.

Taylor glanced over Dakota's shoulder, causing her to

turn and look too. "Camille Rivers. She owns this place."

"The redhead?"

"Uh-huh."

The good news was Dakota figured she would be gone before Frank got back to town. Which meant she wouldn't have to make nice with the woman who was willing to step into the ring with the impossible-to-get-along-with Frank.

But her luck didn't run that true. Camille came with the food. "How does everything look? Is there anything else you need from the kitchen?"

"It looks great." Taylor sank back in her chair to make room for the server delivering her chowder bowl. "Camille, this is Dakota."

Loud and clear in her head, she heard Frank's gruff voice. *Mind your manners, girl.*

Whatever. She didn't often pay attention to anything he said anyway. Nevertheless, it wasn't Camille's fault Dakota had a long-standing feud with the man she was planning to marry.

"Nice to meet you."

"Nice to meet you too. I've heard a lot about you from Frank and Taylor." As they shook hands, Camille's clear brown eyes and a wary consideration did their own assessment.

So, she was a call-it-like-it-was kind of lady. Maybe Camille Rivers could hold her own with Frank. Laney had never been that strong.

"Not all good, I suspect."

"Not all bad, either." Camille smiled. She turned to the others. "I'll have someone come and refresh your drinks."

Happily, after Camille went to greet more customers, the conversation at the table turned quiet as everyone dug into their meals. Dakota joined them because the food was there.

"So, that hotel. Is there one on the beach you'd recommend?" Before Taylor could utter the protest that was clearly coming, Dakota laced their fingers together. "I know you want me to stay with you, but I don't always sleep well at night, and the beach would give me room to roam without disturbing anyone."

Eventually, she'd have to tell Taylor that big sister's job was in jeopardy. Just not yet. And she still had to have the little conversation that had brought her here to Taylor in the first place.

Finally, the kid nodded. "Beachside Inn is nice."

A look passed between Taylor and Leland. Dakota scooted her foot away from the man who'd anchored her and saved her some embarrassment. She didn't know what the look meant, but it didn't bode well, she was sure.

It didn't matter. Her only concern was finding a place to stay for the short time she was in Angel Point and having that talk with Taylor.

Adams finished his sandwich and slung an arm around her sister's shoulders as he stole a spoonful of her chowder.

Dakota mumbled, "I'll check it out. Thanks."

The couple's coziness with each other was kind of cute, and the doc seemed like a nice enough guy, but nice wasn't enough, was it? She'd always figured Laney had started out as a nice enough woman, too, and look how she and Frank had turned out.

So far, from what she'd seen, she was going to have a hard time convincing Taylor to reconsider her engagement. Maybe if she could uncover evidence that Adams wasn't the nice guy he appeared to be . . . Her shoulders slumped. Probably wasn't going to happen. If Gabe had any skeletons in his closet, her sister would have uncovered them by now.

Taylor set aside her napkin and stood. "I've got to head back to work."

Dakota scrambled to her feet. "Want to get together for a drink later?"

"Absolutely. Text me when you're ready."

Adams laced their fingers. "I'll walk you to your truck."

Sitting back down, Dakota scowled. There was no doubt about it. Her mission had landed on shaky ground. A cold nose nudged against her hand, bringing her attention back to the table and Leland.

"He likes you." Leland sounded half-surprised. "I'm ordering dessert. Warm apple pie with a scoop of vanilla ice cream on the side. Want to join me?"

"Thanks, but—" Awkwardly, she patted Tucker's head. Canines weren't her specialty, from lack of experience more than anything, not because she didn't like dogs. "I have to get going."

He stood and held out a hand. As their palms met, Dakota felt a pull in his direction clear to her belly. He might not be Taylor's type, but she suddenly had an insane feeling he could be hers.

Too bad really. She didn't have the time, or luck, in the sexy man department. And because the Marine Corps was hard on relationships, her solution had been not to date, so that now, she was way out of practice.

The seductive smell of apple pie followed her as she forced herself to move with confidence through the scattered tables. Giving the young cashier an extra tip, she wished she could laugh away the idea of her, Dakota James, dating Leland. But face-to-face with the girl's perky smile, she suddenly felt more unraveled around the edges than usual. It was lowering, actually, to be, for the second time in her life, so scrambled, she felt like eggs overcooked, slightly burnt and . . . rubbery.

There wasn't much she could do about that, except live with it. She glanced back at Leland. He was watching, head tilted as if he was trying to figure her out.

Good luck with that.

Leaving the restaurant, she couldn't brush aside the unsettling feeling that Beckett Leland kept watching until she was out of sight.

Chapter Two

LATER THAT AFTERNOON, Beckett could still picture Dakota marching toward him and had to smile. He'd been totally snared by her confident stride, dark hair bouncing around her shoulders, brown eyes snapping as she made her way across the restaurant. At the time, all he could think was . . . *wow!* It was still the first word that came to mind. She was definitely one very provocative lady.

Snuggling Rose, Daisy's daughter, closer, he pushed against the porch, his boot flat against the wood, to keep the swing moving. He gently rubbed his chin over Rose's black hair, taking care not to scratch the baby with the late-in-the-day scruff he never really shaved off.

A cool breeze heavy with the scent of the ocean reminded him he wasn't in Colorado with his family anymore. Colorado, with its mile-high vistas and his concerned parents had made him feel crazy claustrophobic.

Daniel and Joanna Leland came by their hovering naturally, having spent many years taking in dogs retiring out of the military. They were well-known in service dog circles for helping the animals they adopted adjust to civilian life. And they were worried about their son. Beckett got that, so he'd let them talk him into taking Tucker, their newest adoption, with him when he made it clear he wanted to give Angel Point a try.

But so far, the shepherd had shown no interest in anything going on around him. He didn't want to run and play fetch with Preston and JJ. He didn't chase squirrels. No tail wagging. At least not until today when he'd gotten to his feet and sniffed at Dakota's hand.

Beckett had come to Angel Point to pay his respects to his cousin Jason's widow and, while he was at it, to decide what he was going to do with himself now that he was no longer a flyboy in the Marines.

He had to breathe. Figure things out. In that way he agreed with the most determined woman he'd met in a long time. When she'd blurted *You can't marry this . . . this guy!* he'd almost laughed before he realized there was more going on than a simple mistake of identity.

Maybe Tucker wasn't the only one who needed help adjusting to civilian life. Maybe Beckett . . . and Dakota too . . . also needed help in that area. Flying Viper helicopters for the Corps, with multiple tours in Afghanistan under his belt, had left him little time to relax, read a book, take a pretty girl on a date, or think about having a family of his own.

Since coming to Angel Point, he'd discovered he liked being close enough to lend Stacy a hand with her boys when needed. Not that he could take Jason's place, but kids benefited from having a steady guy in their lives to look up to.

A strong sense of belonging and being useful had him more than a little tempted to stay and make Angel Point his home. Almost as tempted as he was to discover why Dakota didn't want her sister to marry the town obstetrician. It seemed to him like the two were a perfect match.

His smile slipped. He could like Dakota, Marine turned U.S. Marshal—according to Taylor—if he wanted to take the time to get to know the lady. She clearly cared what happened to her sister.

Get real, Leland.

Careful not to disturb Rose, he rubbed the ache in his leg where he'd broken it when his Viper went down during his last mission. He shifted his gaze to Tucker. The dog lay at his feet, eyes closed, muscles occasionally twitching. He whined, then gave a soft bark. Dreaming, perhaps, of his own time in the Corps. Beckett's last missions sometimes slipped into his dreams too.

Dakota hadn't stayed for dessert. And at the moment, getting involved wasn't at the top of his bucket list if he was going to make his home in this quaint coastal town.

In any case, if he dated anyone, it would be with the idea of finding someone to spend the rest of his life with. He wasn't a one-night or one-week kind of guy. If he ever got around to looking, he wanted what his parents had. From what he'd seen at the restaurant, Dakota didn't seem to be someone who was in favor of happy-ever-afters.

"Don't you look sexy, rocking that baby girl?" Stacy sat beside him on the swing. "You're going to be a super dad someday."

Stacy worked with Taylor at the sheriff's department, an admin assistant, Jane-of-all-trades. They'd become friends the moment they met. That she didn't object to him hanging out with the boys ironed out some of his restlessness and was one of the reasons he was considering staying in Angel Point. He'd come so close to being one of the unlucky ones. It did his heart good to hold a child who had her whole future ahead of her and to step up to the plate for two boys who missed their dad.

Cuddling Rose closer, he asked, "How was your day?"

"Good. I took a couple of hours off to have lunch at the college with Daisy."

Daisy . . . Rose's mom. Stacy was letting them live in the cottage behind the main house while mama got her GED and a degree in web design.

"How about you?"

"Did you know Jason used to write me letters about Angel Point, you, and the boys?" Soft emotions suddenly filled her eyes in the early evening's soft glow. "Yeah. He told me you guys stayed in touch."

"I've read every one so many times. He made Angel Point sound like the perfect place to live."

"Well, we're not perfect, but it is a great place to raise a family." A note of sadness slipped into her voice.

He wished he could fix that. He admired Stacy and Daisy for their fortitude and determination to build a good future for their families.

One thing he could do was what his parents did, only on a bigger scale. He didn't have all the details worked out but—"I think I've decided to stay. Maybe take in military dogs who are retiring out of the service and help them adjust to civilian life."

"What a great idea. Preston and JJ would enjoy helping you with the dogs. They've loved having you around."

Guilt suddenly stabbed Beckett. He'd made it back. Jason hadn't. With enough regret for both of them, he said, "You've done a wonderful job with the boys."

"That was all Jason." Stacy choked out a laugh. "He loved them both from the moment they were born." Her voice wobbled briefly, but then her chin angled upward. "We've made a good life here. You and your dogs could too. You should go for it."

His dogs. He *should* go for it. He'd moved around a lot while in the Marines. It was time to stop being such a nomad, which meant getting his act in gear and looking around to see if he could find the right property.

An older model white Subaru pulled up at the curb. Daisy hopped out and made a beeline for her daughter. "Was she a good girl today?"

"The best," Beckett reassured the young mother. He handed over the baby. "I'd better get going."

Back at the Beachside Inn, he got out his computer and found a couple of properties that had possibilities. While he was looking, a crazy idea wouldn't leave him alone. Would Dakota consider going on a property hunt with him? Maybe not, after that little mix-up at the restaurant.

It wouldn't be a date. It just would be nice to have a second opinion on the properties. Tucker liked Dakota. Based on what he'd seen at the restaurant, she was super protective of her sister. He would be too, if he had a sibling and he thought that sibling was making a mistake.

You could always trust a fellow veteran.

Tucker stirred by the sliding doors that led to the beach. He sat up, ears forward as he stared out at the water. Putting the computer away, Beckett joined the dog, scratching him between the ears. "Do you want to go for a walk, big guy?"

Tucker stood at attention. As if Beckett's thoughts had conjured her up, along the surf's edge, a lone figure walked. Her cap of dark hair was whipped around by the wind. The sun hung low in the sky. Waves capped white as they somersaulted onto the beach.

He snapped on Tucker's leash and stepped out into the slap of the wind. The shepherd tugged him across a square of grass onto the beach. As he'd suspected, the closer they got to the woman heading toward Shipwreck Rock, the more he was sure the beachcomber was Dakota James. Path meandering, her gaze was locked on the horizon, as if her thoughts took her far from Angel Point.

"Hi."

She whirled around, dark curls flying. Her tawny-brown eyes blinked in surprise. Tucker leaned into the leash, sniffing her hand. She met the dog halfway.

"What are you doing here?" Her eyes widened. "Taylor isn't hurt, is she?"

"I haven't talked to her since lunch, but I'm sure Gabe would call you if she was in trouble." He took the hand she held out to the shepherd. He hadn't meant to make her worry. "I'm staying at the Beachside."

"Does my sister know that?"

"Sure. She recommended the inn to me when I first came to town. Maybe it's her favorite hotel." Reluctantly—which was crazy since he'd only just met the woman—he let go of her hand and resumed walking in the direction she was going when he'd approached her.

"Not likely," Dakota muttered under her breath.

It was true. Taylor wasn't very subtle. He figured the sheriff wanted an extra pair of eyes on her sister, though he didn't know why. He could tell her right now, Dakota didn't appreciate being placed under surveillance.

"So you're staying at the Beachside too?"

She slanted him a cocky side glance. "Taylor's right. It's a nice hotel."

"If you don't mind me asking, why don't you want Taylor to marry the doc?"

She stuffed her hands in her pockets. "How do you know my sister?"

So, she did mind answering questions. Interesting. Dakota picked up her pace. Despite the ache growing in his leg, he managed to keep up."

"Stacy, my cousin's widow, works with her at the sheriff's department."

Tucker wedged himself between them.

"Do you believe so-called love lasts forever?" she asked softly, a faint furrow forming between her brows as she pinned him with an intense stare.

"The truth?"

"Yes."

"I do."

She blushed at his choice of words. "Why?

"My parents have been married thirty-seven years. Whenever they can, they still hold hands. They're perfect together."

"Your parents are an anomaly." She continued toward Shipwreck Rock, watching the seagulls circling the landmark. "It's hard for me to believe there's such a thing as the perfect family. Look at Romeo and Juliet. They did not get a happy-ever-after."

"But then there's Paul Newman and Joanne Woodward," he suggested. "They were married for fifty years."

She rolled her eyes. "Okay, you get a point for that one."

Beckett rubbed his thigh. The movement, more than his defense, caught her attention and slowed Dakota down. Her brows arched with an unspoken question.

"I broke my leg when my Viper went down. It still gives me trouble once in a while."

"You're a Marine pilot." Not a question but acknowledgment, one Marine to another.

"Was," he qualified.

Her unexpected smile kicked him in the gut. "Same here. I mean, I wasn't a pilot, but I was on a Special Reaction Team."

"SWAT team?"

"Yeah." She nodded before turning back the way they'd come.

It was none of his business, but that didn't stop Beckett from asking, "What made you decide to leave the Corps? You were active duty for what? Twelve years? That had to have been a hard decision to make."

"What made *you* leave?"

Fingers of water raced up within a few inches of her feet. Dakota James was one tough cookie. He liked that. Maybe a little too much for his own good.

If they were going to be friends—and he hoped they would, since they had things in common—she should know there had been one thing he couldn't fix. "Too many tours to Afghanistan. The last time, when my Viper went down, we were lucky. Everyone made it out alive. After that, I figured my luck had run its course, so when it was time to reenlist, I didn't."

"Same here. My team responded to an emergency call that could have gone south in a bad way. It was a miracle it didn't. When it came time to reenlist—" She shrugged, the weary look clearing from her face.

"What made you transfer to the Marshals?"

That brought her sculpted brows together. "The U.S. Marshals is in the James family blood."

So they were both starting over. "Will you be in Angel Point long?"

Her fingers buried themselves in the fur along the shepherd's neck. Even more intriguing, Tucker didn't seem to mind. "I'm not sure. Maybe a couple of days," she said as he lengthened his stride to get shoulder to shoulder with her.

The sun trembled on the distant horizon, the last light of the passing day skimming in a pale beam across the water, glinting off mahogany highlights in her hair. Their feet scrunched in the sand and the seagulls cried as they soared overhead.

"Would you be interested in looking at property with me?"

They'd reached the hotel. She looked at him in surprise.

He took in the long stretch of beach ahead of them. "I want to buy some property so I can adopt military dogs retiring from service. I wondered, while you're in town, if you'd like to check out a couple of places with me."

The peace of the sun calling it a day, last rays saying good night across the water, called to Beckett. Just a couple of blocks to the east was Warren Avenue, the main street that ran north and south through Angel Point. This town could be the place for him. Could he expand his idea and maybe pair his dogs with veterans? It was an interesting possibility.

"I'm on the end, second floor." Dakota scratched Tucker's head before shoving her hands in her pockets. "I guess I could help you look for property, if you really want me to."

"Don't sound so excited." He laughed and gestured toward a ground-floor unit. "This is me."

As she backed toward the inn, Tucker whined and tried to follow, stretching the leash until it was taut.

For the first time since Beckett had gotten an eyeful of this force of nature coming his way at The Chowder House, a genuine smile spread across her face. "Tomorrow?"

"I'll let you know what time."

"Night, Tucker." Long strides carried her away.

Beckett squatted beside the shepherd. "What do you think, Tuck? Have we made a new friend?"

Tucker barked once. Beckett swore he heard the dog say, *you bet.*

And friends—human and canine—had each other's backs. She didn't trust him. That much was clear. Maybe he needed a plan to change that. If Dakota helped him with his quest to find a place, there had to be something he could do for her in return.

Chapter Three

S HE SHOULDN'T HAVE agreed to look at property with Beckett, but he'd had that challenging glint in his warm blue eyes when he asked. And there was Tucker. How could she say no? It was no hardship at all to spend a morning or afternoon, or even a whole day with the dog, even if that meant spending significant time with Beckett, too.

Dakota slipped on her pajamas and crawled into bed. Beckett . . . and his dog . . . had definitely made an impression. And not a bad one.

She stared at the ceiling, going over their conversation. He was funny. Honorable. Look at his plans to take in retiring service dogs. Who did that? Beckett, it seemed.

Just because they disagreed on the love leading to happy-ever-after thing, that didn't mean they couldn't become friends, right?

She had Taylor. She had work acquaintances. In boot camp, she'd had two fellow Marines, Mercy Hunter and Paris Roman, who she'd hung out with. She'd lost track of them over the years, but that was natural. They'd each gone their separate ways after graduating.

Yawning, she rolled to her side. It would be nice to have a new friend, someone dependable and trustworthy. Aside from the fact that he had a cool dog, was that why she'd told Beckett she'd go with him?

She stacked the pillows under her head, and for the first time in months, sank into a dreamless sleep.

The next morning, after watching the surf as the sun chased away the night, she texted Taylor. "Breakfast?"

"Meet you at Ginger's Coffeehouse on Warren Avenue in thirty minutes."

Grabbing her keys, Dakota mapped the route on her phone. It wouldn't hurt to get there early to scope out the place. She liked her back to the wall and a clear path out of any building. Always had after Laney left them without a backward look.

Frank was tough. Her drill instructor was tougher. So she'd buried all the churning emotions from her childhood as deep as she could get them, and they'd stayed buried until the lid came off in South Carolina.

That was one of the reasons she'd come to Angel Point. Yes, Taylor had asked her to come. And she did because she wanted to talk the kid into reconsidering a relationship that wouldn't end well. If she couldn't talk Taylor into changing her mind—a long shot, probably, knowing her sister—then maybe she could convince Taylor to opt for a long engagement to be certain of avoiding any fatal matrimonial crashes down the road.

That sounded crazy even to Dakota, but what else could she do? It had hurt so much when their mother had left, not caring that she was abandoning her four and almost six-year-old with a workaholic father who had no idea what to do with the motherless girls.

After losing her emotional whatnot in South Carolina, she'd hoped the job with the Marshals would stop the upheaval rocking her job, her life, everything. But it hadn't taken her long to realize that a change in locale was not going to be her saving grace.

The meltdown should have cost Dakota her job. It was humiliating to be taken off the most important case of her career. No one had ever told her she was off the rails, except Frank. She was lucky Granger had only ordered a leave of absence and that, for some inexplicable reason, he still wanted her on his team.

So here she was trying to make things right for Taylor . . . and herself, while she was at it.

Parking the Mustang on a pretty street near the coffeehouse, Dakota sat for a long moment, wondering what she could say to her sister to make her see reason. Finally climbing out of the car, she leaned on the roof, breathing in the scents of early morning in Angel Point. Salty air just off the ocean. The tempting smell of pasties from a nearby bakery.

She followed the aroma of fresh coffee. A bell tinkled overhead when she entered the coffeehouse. An older lady behind the counter smiled and invited, "Have a seat anywhere."

The place was surprisingly inviting. And busy. But there was an open table back in the corner, against the far wall. She'd barely settled in when Taylor arrived. Her sister's crisp white shirt was tucked into black jeans. A sheriff's star claimed a prominent place on her chest. Black boots, along with a holstered gun at her belt, finished off the image of an old-fashioned, small-town lawman. The look suited the kid.

Taylor stood just inside the door, all business, carefully checking out the room. She looked so much like a feminine version of Frank. Dedicated to the job. That don't-mess-with-me James tilt to her more delicate chin on full display. But there was something different about her baby sister. She seemed less worn around the edges and softer than Dakota remembered.

When Taylor's sharp gaze found her, a huge grin changed her face, making the kid look more like a schoolgirl than the law enforcement officer she was.

Suddenly crushed in an exuberant hug, Dakota returned the favor. She shouldn't have stayed away so long, but she'd been too embarrassed to explain she'd lost the vaunted James cool. It was bad enough that Frank knew.

"It's so good to see you," Taylor whispered in her ear before claiming a seat.

Taylor sat so she could see the door and suddenly Dakota didn't feel so bad. The occupational . . . or more likely, family habit was alive and well in the James girls. "Good to see you, little sister."

"Morning, Sheriff. What can I get you ladies?" asked the woman from the counter.

"Hi, Ginger. This is Dakota James, my sister."

"Nice to meet you, Dakota."

"Ginger owns the coffeehouse."

Thick, gray hair hung past the woman's shoulders. Humor added layers to her brown eyes. She wore a white chef's jacket and what Dakota guessed were black yoga pants, and a sweet smile.

"I'll have eggs, toast, and a vanilla latte," Taylor ordered, not bothering with the menu.

"I'll have the same," Dakota said as her stomach gave a hungry grumble.

Taylor, in her usual blunt manner, got straight to the point. "I asked you to come celebrate my engagement to Gabe, not to try to talk me out of marrying him."

Ginger brought their coffees. "Here you go." Thankfully, the shop owner didn't linger. Dakota didn't like an audience when she was being dressed down.

Wrapping both hands around the warm cup, she shifted onto her elbows. In the back of her mind, she cataloged each patron: young mother, shopper, teacher.

She sighed heavily. This conversation wasn't going to be as easy as she'd thought on the drive north from San Francisco. "I don't want you to make the same mistake Frank and Laney made."

"I'm not making a mistake." Taylor gently manacled Dakota's wrist. "Marrying Gabe is the best thing that's happened to me."

She met Taylor's determined gaze. Surely, it was filled with compassion, not pity. Still—"How do you know?"

"We both saw and lived through what happened between Frank and Laney, but that doesn't mean the same will happen to us. We're smarter than that." Taylor's smile was crooked and gentle and lit up her blue eyes. "Gabe makes me happy, Kodie."

Bullcrap. "How. Do. You. Know, Tay?"

Her sister leaned closer. "I have this warm, giddy feeling deep in my gut, and I have faith in Gabe and me. He's smart. Gentle. Passionate about his work. He makes me want to be a better person. And he's willing to go out on a limb for me—Taylor James, U.S. Marshal-turned-small-town-sheriff." She sighed, apparently coming to a happy conclusion. "I don't want to spend another day without Gabe. And I want you to give him a chance."

"Some people are engaged for, you know, five years or longer."

Taylor's grin, accompanied by the barest shake of her head, doomed Dakota's argument. "Not this someone." Dakota turned her hand so their fingers laced. "Okay. But if this doesn't work out, promise you'll call me?"

"Gabe and I will work out." Taylor squeezed her hand. "I promise."

The food arrived. They ate in silence until Taylor picked up her knife to spread apple butter on her toast. "What's going on between you and Frank? I know you've never really gotten along, but he says you haven't talked in six months."

Frank had seen Dakota at her lowest. A point even worse than when Laney had left. He'd sobered her up and left, but not before giving her a lecture on the state of her life.

"I don't want to talk about Frank."

"Okay, but I think you would really like Camille."

Suddenly desperate to talk about something else . . . anything else . . . before she could bite back the words, Dakota blurted, "I found Laney."

Taylor slowly set her coffee cup aside. "You what?"

"I found her, Tay."

"Did you see her? Talk to her?"

Dakota pressed her lips into a straight line. She hadn't planned on telling her sister so bluntly. Had thought she never would, actually. She could kick herself for carelessly tossing the information at her sister just to save her own pride.

"She wouldn't talk to me."

"Why not?"

"Because—" Dakota sucked in a breath to calm the erratic storm building in her chest. Maybe they both needed to face reality. "She's married and has a teenage kid."

Sadness flickered in the back of Taylor's eyes. For the longest moment, she was quiet, her brows drawn together, but then she met the turmoil in Dakota's gut with a calm Dakota envied. "So, she took a chance on love again."

"I don't know about that, but I can give you her address if you want."

"No, that's okay. I haven't needed to know where she is for a long time." Taylor cocked her head, studying her closely with the James's intensity Dakota knew so well. "Don't you wish her luck with her new family?"

She tried to play nice and almost made it. "I don't know if I can, but I don't wish anything bad for her, either."

For the first time, Dakota meant it, and a piece of the rock that was lodged in her heart flaked off.

Taylor leaned back in her chair. "That's progress, at least." Her wink caught Dakota off guard. It'd been a long time—since they were kids, actually—that her sister's amused approval had made a crack in the wall she'd erected all those years ago.

She'd come to save Taylor. Maybe she was mistaken. Maybe, *she* was the sister that needed saving.

For heaven's sake! How dumb was that?

Taylor was right. Knowing what had happened to Laney didn't change a thing. They'd both come a long way from the frightened little girls Laney had left behind.

Well . . . if she couldn't talk Taylor out of her engagement madness, then maybe she should take advantage of her forced leave of absence to get some beach time in Oahu, where tropical sunshine and some distance from the chaos she'd made of her life promised to set her right.

"Morning, ladies. Mind if I join you?"

Dakota jerked around. Beckett stood there, tall, lean, dressed in close-fitting jeans and a black T-shirt that would draw the most reticent female eye and make her pulse bounce.

She was not that girl.

The man did have a bad habit of sneaking up on her. In more ways than one. It was a first, and she didn't like it. No one ever surprised her to the point that her heart wanted to jump out of her chest.

Before she could articulate a word, like *no*, Taylor spoke for both of them and indicated one of the empty chairs at the square table. "Hey, Beckett, have a seat."

He took the one across from Taylor, which put him next to Dakota. Tucker lay down on the floor between them. Disconcerted, she edged away so the smell of freshly showered man and . . . was that cedar wood? . . . didn't scramble her already-challenged thought processes.

A coffee and breakfast bagel arrived for Beckett. He smiled at Taylor. It was easy to see why she'd thought they didn't suit. Absolutely no sparks. Not that Dakota was glad about that or anything.

Beckett picked up his bagel. "Where's the doc this morning?"

"He's at the hospital delivering twins." Taylor's voice turned soft with pride before she glanced at her watch and scooted back her chair. "I've got to get to work myself."

Oahu was calling. Dakota joined her sister, disturbing Tucker, who jumped to all fours at the same time. "I should go too."

"You haven't finished your breakfast." Taylor exchanged one of those looks with Beckett—they had a bad habit of doing that—and waved her back into her seat. "How long can you stay?"

Sinking back into the chair, Dakota shrugged. "I was thinking of leaving in the next day or two."

"Back to San Francisco?"

"Not exactly." She glanced at Beckett, who was making quick work of his breakfast and acting as if he wasn't listening. Dakota didn't buy it.

Taylor however, had her feet planted. Despite her assertion that she had to get to work, it didn't look like she planned on leaving until she got answers.

"My boss suggested I take some time off."

"Why? What happened?"

Beckett put the unfinished portion of his bagel sandwich back on the plate. They both stared at her. Waiting. *Gawd!*

"I had a little meltdown when a child got in the middle of a drug sting. We'd been working on the bust for a month—" Okay, maybe it was more than a *little* meltdown, but Taylor and Beckett didn't need to know that. "The kid is fine but I was, kind of, asked to take some time off."

She could still hear Granger's words loud and clear.

"You're no good to me if you can't hold it together. Now, get out of here and don't come back until you've got a grip."

He'd pointed at the door, the decision final. No more arguments.

Taylor made a face, which as far as Dakota knew, her sister never did. That face, though, a twist of lips and scrunch of her nose, said enough. "So, where are you planning to go?"

"Oahu."

Taylor stared her down. "How much time do you have left? Have you already gotten your plane ticket?"

Dakota could see why the kid had made sheriff. Criminals wouldn't dare cross Sheriff James when she had that resolute look in her eyes. This was not going to end the way she wanted.

"About ten days and not yet."

She had agreed to look for property with Beckett, but he would understand and let her off the hook if she left before he found anything he wanted to check out.

Taylor wasn't that understanding. "Since you have some time off, I could use your help with planning Camille and Frank's wedding shower. I thought we could host it at my place when he gets back."

Say what?

Before she could protest, Dakota found a finger pointing in her face. She leaned back. "Don't you dare leave tomorrow or the next day without saying goodbye. We'll talk about this later."

And then her baby sister took off in a huff, leaving a trail of frustrated steam behind.

"You do know I'm the oldest, right?" Dakota managed to fling at Taylor's retreating back. The only response she got for that moment of valor was a smirk and wiggle of fingers as Taylor went out the door.

When she came back to earth, there was Beckett, witness to another crazy James scene.

"Your problems keep piling up, don't they?" he dead-panned.

She flushed, dang it. "Which problem would that be? The one where I was told by my boss to take time off and not come back until I had my head on straight? Or the one where my sister is putting me to work on a bridal shower for Frank—who I haven't spoken to in six months, by the way—and his future wife?"

Beckett snorted, a deep sound that went through her like a steamroller.

Nope. Don't go there, James.

"I can see how ticking off the boss and doing a favor for your sister could be problems you don't want to address." Gray-blue eyes were backlit with humor.

Tucker put a paw in her lap as if he sympathized. The dog was cool.

"I need to walk." Dakota grabbed the small backpack she used as a purse.

Beckett didn't argue, but stood to go with her. Whatever.

Leaving the coffeehouse, they went north on Warren Avenue, passing the Dragon Gallery and the Old Town Playhouse. The sky was spotted with clouds overhead.

Angel Point was actually a cute little town. Dakota could hear the ocean in the distance, a low sound she could barely distinguish from the crowd moving around her. She let her mind free fall. She was not going to get all tied in an emotional knot just because Taylor had called her out and backed her into a corner like the old days. Her sister was a very clever woman.

Beckett turned them down a side street away from the busy avenue. The waves got louder. Dakota stepped off the curb. Before she knew what was happening, Tucker crossed her path and leaned against her legs, stopping her right there. Beckett grabbed the dog's collar and Dakota's arm and yanked them both back onto the sidewalk. A car whizzed by at an alarming speed for the pedestrian area.

Her heart pounded. "Oh my God! Is Tucker okay?"

"He's fine. He wasn't hit."

Dakota whipped out her cell and texted the license number to Taylor, with a description of the near accident. When she was done, she bent down to bury her face in Tucker's fur. "Thanks, buddy. You were paying better attention than I was."

She looked up at Beckett. "Thank you for moving so

fast."

"I can when the need arises." Shoving his hands in his pockets, he took a deep breath.

"Well, I'm grateful. It would not have been pretty if that car had hit us." Dakota stood. She owed him one, for sure. "When do you want to look at property?"

"If you're planning to leave town in the next couple of days, the sooner the better." They crossed the street. "I have a favor to ask."

Well, crumbs. She was getting awfully popular all of a sudden. "Sure."

"Tucker likes you."

Curious now, she tilted her head to see Beckett better. "I like him too."

"I wondered if you would keep him for a few days, to help him get used to being a civilian."

She pulled on her earring. "I don't know anything about training dogs."

"But you do know what it's like to have to adjust to civilian life."

He was serious. "Kind of. As you heard, I'm still trying to figure out what that looks like. And I won't be in town long," she reminded him.

He tossed her Tucker's leash. "I'll take however much time you can give him. It will help Tucker a lot. He clearly trusts you."

Dakota had never actually met a knight in shining armor. Not that she was looking. But she would never have guessed that the legendary figure would show up in the form of a former Marine Viper pilot.

He suddenly stopped. "Have you ever flown a kite?"

"No," she said briskly, checking out the store that had captured his attention.

She stepped back to read the sign over the door. Nolan's Kite Shop. Tucker stood at attention, sniffing the air, as if he couldn't figure out why the little shop held so much appeal either. "Tucker doesn't think we need a kite."

"He doesn't? Are you sure?"

She knelt next to the dog; an arm slung around his neck. His fur tickled her cheek. She pretended to listen and couldn't help but smile when Tucker buried his nose in her hair. "Pretty sure."

"Well, I say we get kites, anyway," Beckett said. "My treat." Disappearing into the store, seconds later he stuck his head back out. "Better come inside or you'll end up with a bright purple sea turtle kite."

Taking a firm hold on Tucker's leash, she followed and told him again, "I won't be in town that long."

"Which do you like better, the rainbow octopus kite or this orange sun one?"

The man was impossible. Completely impossible.

Tucker sat on her foot as if that would keep her in town longer than she planned to stay.

Fine. She would let them win this round and stay a few

days longer. If she did, there was a remote—heavy on the word *remote*—chance she might still be able to change Taylor's mind, though she doubted it. At least, she could give it another try.

Snickering, she grabbed the largest, brightest, dragonfly kite she could find and almost beat Beckett to the cash registers.

Chapter Four

WHEN DAKOTA SNATCHED up the dragonfly kite, her expression saying loud and clear she was up for any challenge he tossed her, Beckett finally figured out why he'd felt inspired to pair Tucker with the marshal. He wanted her to trust him, because as much as Tucker needed help with his transition to civilian life, so did Dakota James. He was sure of it.

There was something about her that made him want to do more than sit on the sidelines. As he watched the two advance on him, Beckett had a sneaky feeling they were three of a kind. Maybe they could help each other.

A new idea crystallized in his mind. Finding the right property was the first step, but if he could just keep Dakota focused on Tucker—He picked out two more kites, a black-and-white seagull one for Preston and a bright green frog on white background for JJ.

All he had to do was keep his wits about him and re-member they were partners in this new mission, nothing more.

"I've got this," he said. Dakota didn't have a firm grip on

the kite she'd chosen, so taking it from her was quite easy.

"Hey. I can pay for mine."

Her determination and spunk were so dang appealing but getting pulled into a relationship right now—even a casual one—wasn't part of the plan.

"It was my idea to get the kites," he reminded her, adding her dragon kite to the rainbow octopus one he had chosen for himself and the two he'd picked for the boys.

"Did you find everything you need?" the lady behind the counter asked.

"We did." Beckett pulled out his wallet. "Thank you."

"At least let me pay half."

"How about you pay for coffee next time?" He grabbed the bag of kites and headed toward the door.

Dakota's dark brows came together. If he were a betting man, he would lay down money she was thinking there wouldn't be a next time. He waited as she thought his proposal through. This was going to be good.

"Okay, I'll take you up on that I-owe-you," she said, her expression brightening. "Lois Lane and Superman. Their relationship was doomed from the start."

Beckett nearly dropped the bag of kites the clerk had given him. He could be in big trouble here if he wasn't careful. He countered, "But then there's Aragorn and Arwen of Rivendell. Their love lasted forever."

Once outside, he turned in the direction of the coffeehouse where they'd left their vehicles. When he realized

Dakota and Tucker weren't following him, he turned around.

One hand on her hip, and Tucker sitting at her feet, they were the perfect picture of an Amazon warrior and her best friend. "They're not real people," she argued.

"Neither are Lois and Superman."

"Right." She closed the distance between them. "The point is—"

"The point is, there are lots of examples of love lasting a lifetime. And you're not the only one who wants proof before they take the leap."

She reached him and made a *pfft* sound that went straight into his chest. Their debate revved up his pulse. He wasn't too proud to admit, he was liking how their little game seemed to bring her mistrust closer to friendship. He liked it so much in fact, it made him reckless.

"Do you want to come with me to give these kites to Preston and JJ?" When she hesitated, he had no problem using a little bribery. "We can take your car, if you want." Then added what he knew would be an outrageous suggestion. "Taylor says you have a classic Mustang. Can I drive?"

"Absolutely not." She choked and shook her head. "That car is my baby."

"How long have you had it?"

This time she kept up. "She was my reward for finishing boot camp."

"Sure you won't let me take her for a spin?"

Ignoring him, she looked down at Tucker. "Want to go for a ride, fella?"

Beckett grinned. First round: Leland one. James zero.

IT TURNED OUT no one was home at Stacy's house. Back in the car, the kites in the back seat with Tucker, windows down, Dakota sat for a long moment without starting up the Mustang. She drummed her fingers on the steering wheel.

Beckett ventured a guess, "Not ready to go back to the inn?"

"I'm not really a 'sit around and watch TV' kind of girl. And I don't want to bother Taylor at work." She turned the key. The motor roared to life. "Wanna go for a drive?"

"I was hoping you'd ask."

She looked in the rearview mirror. "How about you, Tucker?"

The dog stuck his head out the window, sniffing the sea air.

"I'll take that as a yes."

Beckett settled comfortably into the seat to enjoy the ride. "When I was a kid, my dad would take my mom and me for a drive every Sunday. It was his way of making sure he spent time with us. How about you?"

She kept her eyes on the road, the blank expression he'd come to know meant she didn't want to talk, springing firmly into place.

He didn't let that kidnap the conversation. "Did you have any family traditions when you were a kid?"

"Not really." She glanced at him, then quickly returned her eyes to the road. "So, you're an only child?"

"Mom couldn't have any more after me."

They drove out of town. Easy silence grew between them before she asked, "Did Taylor ever tell you about our parents?"

"No."

"Our mother left when we were little kids." She spoke so low he almost didn't catch the words.

"I'm sorry. That must have been hard."

She shrugged. "It happens all the time."

He angled to face Dakota. "Not all the time. Is that why you don't believe in love and marriage?"

She kept her eyes on the road. "Physical attraction is too often mistaken for love. Frank and Laney aren't the only example—"

"Of course not." It really bothered him that she'd been hurt by her parents' decisions when she was a little girl with no one to be her defender. "You're not your mom or dad."

"No, you're right. But the odds of staying together as long as your parents have aren't good."

"Perhaps, but don't forget Lucy and Ricky Ricardo. They made their marriage work."

Her smile came back and lit up her eyes. Beckett felt the

win clear down to his boots.

"Yeah, they kept it real." She turned onto Sunrise Road. "Tell me about your parents."

That he was happy to do, and couldn't resist the urge to poke at her a little. "They live in Durango, Colorado. As you know, they've been married forever."

She rolled her eyes. He laughed.

"How did they meet?"

"They were high school sweethearts."

"Risky." She pulled sunglasses from the visor and put them on.

"They never thought so."

Suddenly, she slowed the Mustang just past a pickup on the side of the road. The far side was minus a tire and balancing on a jack. An older gentleman struggled with the tire.

"Not again." She pulled over and parked just ahead of the older model truck.

Beckett twisted to get a better view of the situation. "You know him?"

"We've met."

The guy straightened as they approached.

A genuine smile touched Dakota's lips. "Hi, Claude. Looks like you need to buy new tires."

"I think you're right, Miss Dakota." He patted the tire he was wrestling. "Is this your young man?"

"Nooo. He's not—We're not—"

Spellbound by her sudden self-conscious denial, Beckett held out his hand. "Beckett Leland. How do you know Dakota?"

"Claude Henley." Claude shook Beckett's hand. "She helped out an old man by changing my tire out on Highway 101."

Dakota pinked up. "I was passing by and happy to help." She took the tire from Claude and quickly fitted the rim to the hub hanging in the air.

Charmed by the blush blooming on her cheeks and the ease with which she took over for the older man, Beckett had no problem letting her take point. It was more than a little enchanting, actually. Maybe a little too much.

"Are you kids from around these parts?"

"I'm a recent arrival to town, and Dakota is visiting her sister, the sheriff."

"Sheriff James? Nice lady. Stops by every once in a while to check on me and the missus." Claude nodded at Dakota. "Think we should give her a hand? She wouldn't let me help the last time."

Beckett considered Claude's question for a second as he watched her work, weighing whether he wanted to interfere in her self-appointed task.

"Stay back, Tucker," she ordered the dog.

That answered Claude's question. "Nah."

Five minutes later, she was done and taking the truck off the jack.

A grin spread across Claude's weathered face. "You've got yourself one of those independent types, just like my Betty."

"Yes, sir." Beckett laughed. That was putting it mildly. Not that she was his. He should let Claude know that. "Actually, we're just friends."

"That's too bad, son." Claude winked.

For Pete's sake. A little attraction might be stimulating, but he couldn't take it any further than that.

Dakota picked up Claude's tools. "Do you want these and the jack in the truck?"

"You can put them in the toolbox." Claude gestured toward the back of the truck. "Would you young folks like to come to the house? It's just up the road a bit. I know Betty would like to thank you too. And she always has lemonade and fresh-baked cookies in the cookie jar."

Beckett glanced at Dakota. "That sound okay?"

"Oh, yeah. I've had Betty's cookies. They're the best I've ever eaten."

"Told ya." Claude rubbed his hands together. "Follow me."

Hardly a mile down the road, Claude turned at a mailbox, driving down a long dirt road leading to a white, two-story farmhouse with a dark-green door and shutters. The covered porch could use a little attention, but flowers were in full bloom in the beds out front.

Dakota took the road slowly. "What a beautiful place. Is this what you're looking for?"

"Something like this would do the trick for sure." Beckett took in the picturesque setting.

She parked next to Claude's truck. Beckett let Tucker out, leaving his leash in the car. The dog followed them into the house where they found Mrs. Henley, snowy-white hair pulled into a bun on top of her head, taking a pan out of the oven. Flour dusted her red-plaid apron. On the counter, as if she'd been expecting company, a blue-patterned platter was loaded with cookies.

Beckett hesitated, hand on Tucker's head. Obediently, the dog stayed close. "Is it okay that Tucker came in the house?"

"He's more than welcome. We love dogs." Claude placed a kiss on his wife's temple. "Hi, love. We have guests. This is Beckett Leland and Dakota James. This is the young lady I told you about, who helped me change the tire on the truck yesterday."

"I'll bet you folks are thirsty and hungry. And you're just in time. I just took oatmeal raisin cookies out of the oven." Beaming at them, she handed the plate of cookies to her husband. "Claude, take these to the dining room and I'll bring the lemonade."

"The recipe is her grandmother's," Dakota whispered, then said to their hostess, "Can I help you, Mrs. Henley?"

In the dining room, Beckett went to the picture window, taking in the manicured side yard that was separated from the field beyond by a fence that was a little worse for wear. A large, red barn stood off to the side. If he could find a place similar to this one, he would count himself lucky. There was room enough for what he was planning and maybe even more.

Claude joined him at the window.

"You've got a great place here."

"As Betty and I get older, it's hard to keep up with everything, but we wouldn't live anywhere else."

"What are you men up to over there?" Betty asked with a contented smile as she placed a tray of glasses on the table. Dakota followed with a large pitcher of lemonade.

Claude smiled tenderly at his wife. "We were just admiring the view."

Beckett filled a glass with lemonade. "You have a lovely home, Mrs. Henley. I can see why you and Claude like it so much."

Betty took the glass he offered. "We've spent a lot of good years here."

They all settled around the table. Claude poured three more glasses of lemonade. "You kids ever in the military?"

"Marines," Beckett said at the same time as Dakota, then helped himself to a cookie after she'd taken one. "How can you tell?"

Claude raised his glass in salute. "Army Ranger. Korea. I can always spot another veteran."

Tucker prowled the perimeter of the room. Beckett nudged Dakota's foot and angled his chin toward the restless dog.

Dakota patted her thigh. "Come here, Tuck."

"What a handsome dog." Betty leaned over, holding out her hand as Tucker drew close. The dog sniffed her fingers but edged cautiously past the older woman to get to Dakota.

"Don't hold his cautious nature against him, Betty. Staff Sergeant Tucker just retired from the Marines. He was a bomb sniffer and is still not accustomed to civilian life. We're working on that."

Claude launched into stories about his time in Korea. Dakota had slipped off her shoe and was rubbing Tucker's back with her foot.

Beckett couldn't help watching. She was completely relaxed. It made him want to take off his boot to play footsie with the intriguing woman.

Claude poured more lemonade in his glass, then raised the pitcher toward Dakota in silent question. She shook her head and patted her stomach. "I think I've had enough."

Beckett wasn't ready to leave. He was having too much fun watching Dakota in what was probably an unfamiliar environment. In San Francisco, he'd bet she had an apartment or condo. How did it stack up next to this country farmhouse?

"Do you have children who come to visit?" he asked to keep the conversation going. Hopefully, the Henleys wouldn't consider the query too intrusive.

Claude shook his head. "We were never that lucky, but

we're happy anyway."

What a shame. Having family to help them around the place would make things easier for the older couple.

Beckett finally stood. "We should get going. Before we do, do you mind if we take a walk around outside?"

"Go ahead, if you don't mind exploring on your own. I'm going to help Betty clean up. Then I think we'll take a little nap."

Beckett had noticed Betty's shoulders drooping, but she straightened at the sound of her husband's voice. "Don't be silly. I'm not a child. I don't need a nap."

"Of course, but I feel a nap coming on, and I was hoping you'd join me." Claude winked, holding a hand out to his wife.

A soft smile evened out the lines of her face. "You're such a charmer."

Dakota grabbed the glasses. "I'll take care of the kitchen."

"Just put the dishes in the sink," Claude instructed.

Betty tucked her hand in the crook of Claude's arm and leaned into his shoulder. "You're a good husband, Claude Henley. What would I do without you?"

Beckett could tell by the look on Claude's grizzled face, the feeling was mutual.

Dakota carried the dishes to the kitchen. Beckett grabbed what was left, and the platter with the few remaining cookies, and followed.

"Nice couple."

"Don't tell me how long they've been married," she warned.

He buried his grin. "I don't actually know but probably they've been together—"

"Forever," Dakota finished his sentence.

"How about that walk now?"

"Okay." She wiped her hands on the dish towel he'd been using before draping it over the edge of the sink. "Tucker needs to stretch his legs before we put him back in the car."

The back porch ran the width of the house. The barn was imposing, but at the same time had a well-used air about it. Walking across the grass to the fence, he pointed out a smaller enclosed structure close to the barn. "Looks like they had chickens at one point."

He turned and leaned against the wooded rails, his elbows on the top plank. The back of the house was as picturesque as the front.

"What are you thinking?"

What was he thinking? "I'd love to find a place like this one. It's sad that Claude and Betty never got the chance to raise a family here."

Dakota went still. Tucker halted his exploration of the fence line. She blurted out of the blue, "Frank's not my father."

Before he could think of a response, she spun and stalked

around the house to the front where the Mustang was parked. "Tucker, come!"

She was in the car and seat belted in before he caught up. Claude watched from the front porch.

Beckett altered course, taking the porch steps two at a time. The Mustang's engine roared impatiently to life. He held out a hand to the older man. "Thanks for letting us spend the afternoon."

Claude shook his hand, nodding in Dakota's direction. "She might be a spitfire, but she's a keeper. Both of you come visit again."

"We'll definitely try," Beckett promised.

He jogged to the revved-up car and barely got his seat belt latched before she released the brake.

He had a spitfire? A keeper? Not likely.

"So, Frank isn't your father? Does Taylor know?"

She wouldn't look at him. Still, he noticed she was careful not to beat up the Mustang on the dirt road on the way out.

"No." She didn't elaborate.

His original plan had been to help Tucker. Then he'd met Dakota. Maybe his plan had to be bigger. Maybe what he wanted was to help all veterans—canine and human. Would Dakota let him help her?

If he wanted her to trust him, which he did, more than anything now, he was just going to have to come up with a plan and try harder.

Chapter Five

DAKOTA WOKE TO the weight of a dog's paw and nose on her outstretched arm. The soft whine didn't clarify why she had a furry guest in her apartment. It took her a minute to remember she wasn't in San Francisco and that Beckett Leland had somehow maneuvered her into keeping Tucker for a few days.

How in the heck did she get herself into these messes?

Beckett had dropped her and Tucker and a big bag of dog food off at the hotel last night, then immediately left with a parting, "Don't forget we have a date for a kite-flying lesson."

And before dropping her off, he'd talked her into exchanging cell numbers.

"Why do you need my number?"

"You have Tucker."

As if that was enough to explain his request. Probably it did. But now, he could call whenever he wanted. She wasn't sure what she thought about that. She hadn't come to Angel Point to make nice with the local dudes, even one as attractive as Beckett Leland.

She should have given more consideration to this so-called mission to talk her sister out of her hasty engagement. Instead, she'd impulsively driven all the way from San Francisco, where she was beginning to make a home, for a conversation that was probably already over.

She snorted. *Date Beckett? Not likely.*

She might like the man and be impressed with his determination to make a difference for his dogs, but she had her own problems to attend to.

Tucker whined again.

"Okay, big boy." She dragged herself to the bathroom. "Let me get dressed."

As soon as she opened the sliding door, the dog dashed out, did his business, and came right back. She scratched him between the ears. "You're a good boy, aren't you?"

Besides, she didn't need to go on a date to learn to fly a kite. She could figure that one out for herself. Beckett probably wasn't serious, anyway.

Filling her lungs with fresh ocean air, for the first time in longer than she could remember, she looked forward to the day ahead. She was ready to head out to take Tucker for a long walk, when a knock broke the comfortable quiet. Dakota opened the door. Taylor pulled her into a tight hug. "Hey, Sis."

How convenient was that? Feeling a little bit crushed and cornered, she let her sister into the room. "Did I know you were coming? Is Gabe with you?"

If he was, it would give her a chance to quiz him and see if he was authentic and as much in "love" as Taylor said she was.

"He's at the hospital, so I thought I would bribe you with doughnuts and steal you away to my place."

"He's working? Sounds like he's a workaholic like Frank."

Taylor laughed. "That's not it at all. He takes plenty of time off, believe me. You just can't go to the store and pick a baby off the shelf when you decide it's time to have a child. They come when they are darn good and ready, no matter what day you plan for them to be born."

"If you say so." It was still very suspicious that the last two out of three times she'd been with Taylor, the fiancé had been noticeably missing.

"Come on. Stop brooding and grab your bag. It's time we started planning Camille's bridal shower. Doughnuts and coffee are on me." Taylor shook the paper bag she carried.

"Hold your horses, kid. Why do I have to help? I won't even be here for the party." Dakota didn't want to do any favors for Frank. It was his fault Laney had left. And it was because of his intervention in South Carolina that she'd started thinking about how lonely she was, despite her structured military life.

"Isn't it about time you stopped calling me kid? I brought your favorites: apple fritter and a caramel latte." *The kid* shot her a *don't-mess-with-me* glance that would have instantly changed Dakota's mind if what Taylor wanted had nothing to do with Frank. "You *will* help me." And then she winked. "Please?"

Her mission to talk some sense into Taylor hadn't changed her sister's mind one iota. At least an impromptu coffee klatch would give her another chance.

Taylor had done her best to look after Dakota while they were growing up, a role reversal she'd unsuccessfully fought until she left home at eighteen. Once Taylor's mind was made up, there was no altering the kid's course.

If Dakota hadn't already known that, it had become abundantly clear when Taylor started calling, supposedly to "check in" every week or so. The kid was good at putting her sisterly nose in where Dakota didn't want it.

All this *let's make up with Frank* talk, insisting she had to have help with bridal showers, bribing Dakota with apple fritters, and the best coffee ever . . . She took another breath. It was kind of nice.

"Okay, but I want you to know I'm giving in under duress," she offered the obligatory resistance, grabbed her wallet and stuffed it with her cell inside her serviceable crossbody bag. "You don't mind if Tucker comes? I'm keeping him for a few days for Beckett."

That was putting it mildly for how the dog had been dropped into her lap. Not literally, of course. As she looked back on it, she hadn't really offered that much opposition. It helped that she liked the dog. What a wuss she'd turned into.

Taylor grabbed the leash from the desk and clicked it onto Tucker's collar. "Of course, I don't mind. There's a park across the street from the duplex where we can take him for a walk when we're done planning the shower."

It wasn't a long ride to the Craftsman Taylor had told her Gabe had turned into a duplex. But every second was filled with old memories that agreeing to work on a bridal shower for Frank's new woman dredged up.

Taylor had been asleep in the bed they shared when the shouting started. Dakota had crept to the top of the stairs.

"*Dakota's your daughter,*" Frank had shouted.

"*I can't take her! You've pretended all this time that she's yours. You keep her.*"

She'd been right to be afraid after hearing what no kid should hear. Laney left the next day, taking neither of her daughters with her. Dakota had waited, in vain it turned out, for her mother to say, "Come on, Dakota, you're going with me," but in her young heart, she knew. Nobody wanted a quiet, scrawny kid who'd had a hard time going by the rules from day one. Not Laney. Not Frank. Only Taylor.

Since that day, she'd tried her best to be a good rule follower. No matter how hard she'd tried, she never gotten the hang of it. And now, with her emotions all over the place, she'd made a wreck of everything.

"You're awfully quiet."

Dakota twisted to face Taylor. "If I asked nicely, would you—?"

Taylor could always read her mind. She covered Dakota's hand, squeezing gently. "There's no doubt in my mind that Gabe and I are doing the right thing. I love him with every molecule I have. And . . ."

Dakota sat up straighter. "What?"

"You'll find out sooner or later. Gabe has leukemia." She hastily added, "It's in remission."

Dakota knew it. Gabe would leave Taylor in the end. Maybe not the same way Laney had left, but the results would be the same. "Then why?"

"Because it's likely he'll be in remission for a very long time, probably until he's an adorably wrinkled old man. Even if that weren't true, I'd rather have a single month or day or hour with Gabe, than to have no time at all with the man I love."

"You...you can't really believe that," Dakota stammered. Why would anyone voluntarily sign up for that kind of emotionally hazardous duty?

"I absolutely do," Taylor said without hesitation. "And, Kodie, if you say a single word to him that changes his mind, I'm telling you now, I will never, ever speak to you again. It was hard enough to convince him to take a risk on us."

Break Taylor's heart by protecting her sister or forever lose the only family she had? There was no contest. Her baby sister was the toughest, bravest person Dakota knew. She had no choice. She would do as Taylor asked and be there if ever the other shoe dropped.

"Okay, I won't say anything."

"Thank you." Taylor squeezed her hand again, then returned to her driving. "I think eventually you'll love him as much as I do. The man grows on a person."

Dakota snorted. "Well, I won't love him as much as you do—that would be kinky—but I do promise to be a good sister-in-law."

"I know you will." Taylor parked the truck. "Now, let's take this conversation inside and gorge ourselves on fritters and coffee."

"All right, kid." Dakota laughed at her sister's scowl and opened the back door for Tucker. "Come on, boy."

Once inside, while the shepherd checked out every inch of the duplex, Dakota had her own look around. Taylor's style was uncluttered lines, a few choice furniture pieces, and occasional color to pop the senses.

She offered an olive branch. It wasn't much but—"I'm sorry it's been so long since I've come to see you."

"You're here now. That's all that matters." Taylor smiled and took their goodies to the kitchen.

"It's just that—" Dakota stopped roaming, stalling out in front of a framed picture taken when they were teenagers.

Frank had taken the photo. Dakota remembered the day as clearly as if it were yesterday. He'd managed to get a rare day off from work to take them on a picnic. On a bench where she could see for miles, they ate the lunch they'd packed at home.

That day, she'd thought, maybe, she could pretend she'd never heard Frank and Laney's heated argument. But the picnic at the park had turned out to be the highlight of her relationship with Frank. From there, it'd all gone downhill.

"No worries, Dakota," Taylor said, coming from the kitchen.

If that were only true. She shook herself loose from the self-pity she hated indulging in, noticing there was nothing of Gabe in the living area. She joined her sister. "You and Gabe aren't living together?"

"We have a connecting door. Does that count?" Taylor handed her a plated apple fritter and one of the coffees. "For the shower, we can open the door and use both spaces. Gabe won't mind."

They sat at the table. Tucker settled by the door. "When are you thinking of having this shower?"

"Ideally, I'd like to have it before you go back to San Francisco. That doesn't give us much time, so I figure we can keep it simple."

They ate their fritters in silence until Dakota gave in to the inevitable. She'd never planned any kind of get-together, shower or otherwise, so didn't have a clue where to start. Except there was that time when she'd heard several Marines planning a party at the club on base. Did eavesdropping count for some kind of experience?

"Who are we going to invite to this shindig?"

"Mostly friends."

"No family?" The lady she'd met at The Chowder House didn't look like someone who didn't have the full support of a family. Not that Dakota knew what that might look like, and looks could be deceiving.

Taylor stopped the piece of apple fritter she'd broken off midway between the plate and her mouth. "Camille has never mentioned family."

"So no stepbrothers or sisters when she and Frank get married?" Okay, she didn't have to say that like it was the worst thing that could happen. Still, this was something that would be good to know.

"I guess not." Taylor polished off her fritter. "Look, I know Frank can be a pain in the backside, but he's trying. Just give him a chance."

Sure. Why not? Not going to happen.

"Do we need a theme for this party?" According to the Marines she'd overheard, they did.

"Good idea."

Taylor leaned back in her chair, studying her closely. It was a bad family trait. Analyze your opponent until you had them figured out and right where you wanted them. Dakota refused to squirm. Nothing to figure out here.

Finally, Taylor said, "How about a Paris theme? Frank wants to take Camille to Paris for their honeymoon. It would be harder to recreate here than say, a beach theme, but I think it's unique and doable."

"We can order stuff online," Dakota suggested. She never went anywhere without her laptop.

"Another good idea. You look for decorations and paper plates and cups. I'll get the cake. I know a guy." Taylor named a day for the party.

Dakota was about to ask about gifts—what did you get two grown people who probably had everything they needed in the household department?—when Taylor stood and said, "Let's take that walk in the park."

Once outside, Tucker pulled on his leash. They walked in silence around the block, looping back to the empty park. "I'm . . . uh . . . glad you hijacked me. That apple fritter was the best I've ever had."

Taylor knelt down to hug Tucker. "Ever?"

"The best," Dakota said sitting on one of the swings, the first free grin since coming to see her sister sneaking out. "So where is this *wedding* taking place?"

"Mine?"

"No, Frank's." She still couldn't believe two out of the three Jameses were getting hitched, practically at the same time. "Wait. Are you having a double wedding?"

Taylor snorted, sitting in the next swing over. "No. Frank and Camille are in a hurry. They want to get married at the end of this month. Gabe and I want a fall wedding."

She was so not jealous! "Have they chosen a venue?"

Tucker dropped to the ground, off to the side and out of the way. Dakota pushed off with one foot. Taylor kicked her swing into parallel motion.

"They wanted to get married at the Second Chance Bed-and-Breakfast, but we had a bad storm last month that took off part of the roof and left a lot of debris laying around the grounds. It'll take a while to get the repairs and cleanup done, so in the meantime, the grand opening has been postponed." Taylor took a breath, then said with a sideways look, "Camille wants us to be her bridesmaids."

Saved by her vibrating cell, Dakota stopped swinging and pulled the phone out of her bag to prevent the *heck, no* trying to get past her clamped lips.

The text could be from her boss, realizing he'd made a grievous mistake by taking her off duty. Being called back to work would be the perfect solution for getting her out of reach of Taylor's party planning.

"Where are you right now?"

"Who is it?" Taylor leaned toward her.

Dang it! Not her boss, but maybe the next best thing. "Beckett."

She texted back. "At Taylor's."

"Don't go anywhere. I'll be right there."

Exactly what she'd been afraid of when she'd given the man her number. That he could contact her whenever he wanted. This time though, she wouldn't mind making a getaway, and she sure as heck didn't care that Beckett Leland would be her getaway driver.

"So, about being Camille's bridesmaid," Taylor persisted.

Because it was Taylor asking, Dakota had to figure out

how to deal with Frank in a way that didn't make her teeth grind. And, at the same time, not reveal how devastated she'd been to find out he wasn't really her dad, that he didn't *want* to be her dad. And because she hated the self-pity that swamped her when she thought about it, no way was she going to tell her sister. Ever.

How humiliating would that be if the kid joined in her pity party, then had to set big sis to rights, just like Frank had?

Everyone gather around and witness the fall of U.S. Marshal Dakota James.

"Hey, I know a couple of single guys I could introduce you to. While you're in town, we could double date. Me and Gabe. You and—"

Dakota was speechless for all of a single nanosecond, then burst out, "No. Nope. Don't you dare."

Taylor burst out laughing.

Just in time, Beckett pulled up in an older Bronco. Dakota could kiss the guy for being so prompt.

Beckett had two boys with him. He turned off the motor, got out of the vehicle, and waved her over.

Sliding her cell back in her bag, she grabbed Tucker's leash.

"So, no blind dates." Taylor snickered. "But how about the bridesmaid gig?"

"I don't know." Dakota sighed heavily. "I'll think about it, okay?"

"Good. Having you at the wedding would mean a lot to Frank and Camille."

Dakota doubted that, but she wasn't going to be the one to say so.

Beckett let Tucker in the back with the kids as he made introductions. "Boys, this is Marshal Dakota James. These two rascals are Preston,"—he indicated the older boy, then handed the younger one Tucker's leash—"and JJ."

"Nice to meet you, ma'am," Preston responded in a tone that said Mom had given orders to mind his manners. Dakota was impressed, but touched too. The boy had no guile in his direct gaze.

Managing to keep a straight face after her sister's teasing about double dating—Taylor had to be giving her a bad time, right?—she shook hands with both kids. "Nice to meet you, boys."

Taylor waved as they pulled away from the curb. Dakota should have been relieved that Beckett had managed to extract her from the uncomfortable scenario of seeing herself on a date with a complete stranger. It wasn't how she envisioned spending her time in Angel Point. But she had a sneaky feeling she'd just jumped from the frying pan into the fire.

"Is there an emergency?" She snapped on her seat belt. "Where are we going?"

"We're going to fly our kites," JJ said, giving a little bounce.

"Not looking at property?" Dakota lifted her eyebrows at Beckett.

"Not today."

She wasn't sure she liked the smug smile he cast her direction. "I seem to have misplaced my kite."

"It's in the back with the boys'."

Wasn't she the lucky one? Yup, she'd definitely jumped into the fire. "What happened to your truck?"

"I need a vehicle with more room for passengers and dogs, so I traded it in for this thing. What do you think?"

What did she think? There was more to Beckett than she'd thought at first.

She looked around the interior. It was in excellent shape for an older model. "I think it should work fine for your dogs."

"My thoughts exactly." He parked in a nearly empty lot close to the sand.

As soon as the Bronco stopped moving and Dakota got out of their way after letting Tucker out, Preston and JJ jumped to the ground. From the back hatch, Beckett handed each their kite, then came around with two more.

As he handed over the dragon kite, she looked longingly up the beach toward the inn. She could just see it in the distance. She passed Beckett Tucker's leash. "If it's okay, it's been a crazy day. I could really use some down time."

He gave the leash back along with a don't-give-up-now look. "Normally, I wouldn't put up an argument, but the boys have been looking forward to flying their kites all morning. And there's two of them and only one of me."

Despite his pushiness, she liked Beckett. She liked that he cared so much about Preston and JJ and wanted to give them a good time. How often did that happen, adults putting kids first? And she liked that he had a plan for Tucker and other retiring dogs like the shepherd.

JJ raced back, stopping inches in front of Dakota, looking up at her with sweet, blue eyes. "Are you really a marshal?"

She didn't know if Beckett was for real, but she couldn't resist the kid's enthusiasm. "I am."

"Will you help me with my kite?"

How could she say no? "Hang on just a second, kiddo."

She bent over to take off Tucker's leash and realized the dog's tail was tucked between his legs. His ears were laid back. He was shaking.

Keeping her voice low and steady, she sat on the sand next to Tucker. "What's up, big boy?"

"What's wrong?" Beckett squatted next to them.

"He's not feeling good."

Tucker let her pull him into her lap, laid his head on her shoulder, and nearly knocked her over. For an awkward moment, she groped for his collar to keep from falling.

At the last minute, Beckett caught her, and she landed against his chest. Strong arms wrapped around her waist. For a silly heartbeat, she got lost in his stormy blue gaze. His lips were close. They twisted to one side in a tempting smile that invited her to join in. Another few inches and she could—

"I . . . uh—" She started to wiggle free, a little breathless, which was crazy, right? Just because she was wrapped in Becket's strong arms and liked the feel of the tempting man around her, didn't mean she could give in and swoon like one of those girls in a 1930's romantic comedy.

She cleared her throat. "I should take him back to the inn."

Tucker, not Beckett.

"That's probably a good idea." Beckett helped her up.

Sucking in a deep breath to even out the erratic beat of her heart, she leaned down to JJ. "Is it okay if I help you another day? Tucker's not feeling well. He needs to eat . . . and take a nap."

The worried look on the little boy's face erased whatever was going on between her and Beckett. She ruffled his hair. "He'll be okay. I promise."

Not looking to see if Beckett had been as affected as she was when she'd landed squarely in his lap, she waved in his general direction and flung out, "See you boys later."

He was a good guy. He had a lot of patience. And plans for his life—a lot more than she did—and he had a lot to offer a woman. She sternly reminded herself . . . it just happened she wasn't that woman.

Chapter Six

A T STACY'S HOUSE, Beckett helped Preston and JJ with the model car kits he'd brought them, partly to spend some time with the boys and partly to take his mind off the shocking moment when Dakota James had landed right in his lap. Sparks had flown in every direction as all his suddenly awakened senses were hot-wired by a lightning bolt of startling awareness.

That was three days ago. And he'd been worrying ever since. His body still pinged at finding the stunning woman wiggling to get off the hard cushion of his alert boy parts. He might be crazy, but it seemed like she'd only started to retreat after a long moment in which he sincerely, and foolishly, hoped they were on the same page.

Her long silence proved they weren't. He could fix this. If she'd just contact him.

Kissing a pretty lady, even a marshal as astute and perfect—well, maybe not totally perfect—as Dakota, didn't even make the top three on his urgent priorities list. And there had been no indication she was interested in being on the receiving end of a kiss. Even though she'd been painfully slow in removing herself from his going-up-in-flames landing pad.

Should he rethink the kissing part?

No! Of course not.

She didn't need him drooling over her like a randy teenager. And she didn't need his poor efforts to "fix" her, though if he could find a solid way to give her a hand with whatever was making things difficult for her in San Francisco, shouldn't he give it a try?

He shook his head. What she needed from him was friendship. A pal who was there when she needed someone at her back. She needed his support no matter what decision she made about her future.

"Cousin Beckett, do these two fit together?" Preston held out the Firebird car body in one hand and what appeared to be a fender in the other.

"Looks like it. Let me help you with that." A little glue and the two parts were bonded together.

His thoughts flew straight as an arrow back to Dakota. Despite his preoccupation with the marshal, she hadn't mentioned settling down and raising a family. Not that it was any of his business.

At least, it didn't appear she had aspirations in that regard or a boyfriend waiting back home.

Exhibit one: her ideas about love and marriage. Exhibit two: the lap dance. Once she got moving, she'd jumped up quicker than his Viper in a super-fast takeoff.

JJ pulled on his sleeve. "Cousin Beckett, Cousin Beckett, can you help me too?"

"Sure, buddy. Hand me your box." He took the Camaro kit from the boy, slipped off the clear wrap. "Clear off that end of the table, and then you can lay out all the pieces."

He glanced at the wall clock. It was midafternoon. He should have heard from her by now. To be fair, later that night after their close encounter of the personal kind, she'd texted to tell him Tucker was better. He'd left them alone, in part so they could get used to being with each another. But he'd thought she would contact him when she realized he wasn't going to make something out of their brief, sexy contact. His only reward was silence from her end.

He gave JJ a hand separating the Camaro parts into sections. The kit was probably too old for a five-year-old, but JJ always wanted to do whatever his older brother was doing.

Beckett kept it simple. He just wished he could take his own advice. "Put all the big parts over here and the smaller ones here."

Before coming to Stacy's this morning to watch the boys while she worked, he'd given in and texted Dakota. Shortly after, she'd texted back. All she'd said was she and Tucker were heading up Highway 101 to Astoria.

It was a thirty-seven-minute drive from Angel Point to Astoria. He'd checked. But she hadn't mentioned she planned to be gone all day. That was no big deal, right? At least Preston and JJ were a great distraction.

Besides, Dakota knew better than most how to take care of herself. And she had Tucker with her. They would take care of each other. Hadn't that been the plan in the first place?

So he'd taken the opportunity to look at a couple of places but hadn't found anything that knocked his socks off. Maybe that would change when Dakota returned and they could look together.

"Cousin Beckett? Can I ask you a question?" Preston's tone was quiet and serious.

Beckett shifted until he faced the kid. "Absolutely. What do you want to know?"

"Um, it's about a girl." Preston's face turned red.

Wasn't it always?

"There's this girl at school and I really like her, but she doesn't like me." Preston dropped his chin, staring at the partially finished body of the Firebird he'd glued together. His small hands turned it over and over.

Beckett showed JJ how to snap together the Camaro body parts, ignoring how easy it was to slot himself in Preston's shoes. He wasn't sure Dakota liked him, either. At least that wasn't part of their agreement. She *was* taking care of Tucker, but only after he'd insisted she keep the shepherd for a few days, an experiment on his part. Still, a girl who didn't like a guy wouldn't take care of his dog, would she?

"So what do you want to know?"

"How do I make her like me?"

Beckett laughed. "You're asking the wrong guy, dude. I wish I knew."

"How do *you* get girls to like you?"

How indeed? What would it take to get Dakota to like him?

Scratch that.

"Well, girls like flowers. If you asked her what her favorite flower is, you could draw a picture of the flower and give it to her."

Preston brightened up. "She has these white flowers with yellow centers on her notebook."

"Daisies?"

The nine-year-old nodded emphatically.

JJ tugged on his sleeve. "What about me? Would Marshal Dakota like it if I draw her a bunch of flowers?"

Leave it to a five-year-old to bravely jump in where grown men feared to tread. The last time Beckett had given a girl flowers was when he was in high school and deep in the throes of his first crush. He was a sophomore. The girl, Karen Markle, was the junior class president. He'd given her a bunch of pink tulips at the spring dance—because what girl didn't like pink?

She'd gently thanked him, but told him she already had a boyfriend who was a student at the local community college. His young heart had come out of his first foray into love pretty bruised. Because of that, he kind of understood where Dakota was coming from. Except, it didn't compare to being abandoned as a small child by divorcing parents. And, she'd be the first to tell him he was overstepping his bounds.

What if she didn't get past that early heartbreak?

"I think she would like that very much, buddy." He tousled the boy's hair.

JJ immediately ran to get drawing paper and crayons. Smiling at the intensity of the kid's concentration and the tongue that peeked out from the corner of his mouth when he got back to the table, Beckett put the bits and pieces of his Camaro model back in the box.

He chuckled as an idea came to him and he texted, "Han Solo and Leia Organa. Great love story."

He checked the time again. Three twenty-seven p.m.

"Leaving Astoria now." Then, "Rhett Butler and Scarlett O'Hara. Couldn't make it work." Followed by an emoji sticking its tongue out.

Grinning, he texted back, "Any problems? Did you have a nice time?"

It took a long minute, but she finally responded with, "Yes. See you soon."

That worked. Suddenly, he had an idea. "Meet me at Stacy's?" He gave her the address. "I'm thinking we'll visit the Henleys."

"Be there in thirty-five."

She'd enjoyed their last visit, for the most part. And Claude might know of some properties for sale. He clapped his hands together. "Okay, boys. Let's clean this place up so your mom doesn't have to do it when she gets home. Then, as soon as Marshal Dakota gets here, we're going for a ride."

Preston and JJ scrambled to put their things away. Beckett let Stacy know he was taking the kids out. In short order, the house was spotless and the three of them were waiting for Dakota on the porch.

She didn't keep them waiting. When she stepped up to the porch, Tucker laid down at her feet, tongue hanging out as he took quick doggy breaths. "I assume we're taking your vehicle?"

"Yup." He took his keys out of his pocket. "Let's load up, guys."

Showing excellent restraint, if he did say so himself, Beckett waited until they were leaving town before he asked questions. "So, how was Astoria?"

"Sweet town," was all she said as she watched the passing scenery.

Deciding it was best not to poke the she-bear, at least for now, he kept quiet and followed the same roads they'd taken on Saturday.

She finally twisted to face him. "I did some research, and we're trying some different relaxing techniques."

"You or the dog?"

She smirked. "Both. I guess. I know I don't have any experience with dogs, and I should have asked, but I thought it might help Tucker after I go back to San Francisco."

Tucker was more at ease as he sat between the boys, JJ's

WANTED BY THE MARSHAL

arm wrapped around his neck. Beckett wouldn't say the same for Dakota. He had his work cut out for him before she headed back home. Frankly, he appreciated the reminder. Their time together was finite.

"No worries."

"Why are we going to the Henley's?"

Beckett slowed to a crawl. "To ask Claude if he knows of any properties for sale."

He parked by the house. Each time he drove up the driveway, he could see himself sitting on a similar porch, with dogs and teenage versions of Preston and JJ. Maybe another child or two. A wife. Not Dakota.

It was a stirring picture, but was it enough?

They were just getting to the porch when a thin scream came from inside the house. Beckett took the steps two at a time, knocked once before entering. "Claude? Betty?"

"In the kitchen," came Claude's strained voice.

The kitchen smelled like fresh-baked bread. He found Betty down near the stove. Claude was attempting to help her sit up.

Beckett squatted next to them. "What happened?"

"I'm so clumsy." Betty leaned against Claude. "I slipped."

"Do you hurt anywhere?"

Claude patted her shoulder. Betty shook her head. "I don't think so."

"Okay then, let's see if you can stand." Beckett checked

to make sure JJ and Preston were out of the way.

The sight of Dakota holding them back against the wall, an arm around each boy as she tucked them tight to her sides, a mama bear protecting her young, if he didn't already have one lady to help, he would go right to her. The kids wore scared faces. Dakota whispered reassurances. Tucker lay at their feet, a resolute barrier between the three and the accident by the stove.

Beckett shot them a wink, then with Claude on Betty's other side, helped her stand. "Oh! My ankle."

Gingerly, they lowered her back to the floor. Beckett pulled out his cell. "I'll call nine one one."

Betty's face crumbled. "Don't do that. I just need a minute to catch my breath."

"It's okay, love." Claude sat on the floor and pulled his wife against his chest. "We need to find out if your ankle's broken."

Beckett punched in the number and said to the operator who answered, "We have a lady down, possible fractured ankle." He gave her the address.

Pocketing his phone, he caught Claude's eye and said softly, "The ambulance is on its way."

Betty sucked in a ragged breath. "I don't want to go to the hospital."

"I know." Claude's arms tightened around her, a look of worry deepening the creases fanning out from his eyes.

Beckett understood. Claude and Betty had been together

for a lifetime. He should be so lucky with his own future wife. His gaze went straight to Dakota.

Back the truck up, Leland.

Dakota had other plans than hitching her ride to a guy's in sickness and in health, for all the years they could be together.

"We'll get out of the way and wait on the back porch," Dakota said quietly, then retreated. "Come on, Tucker."

Beckett wanted to follow. Dakota James might not believe that families could be strong and weather the hard times, as well as the good, together, but he'd take her on his team any day of the week. Hiding beneath all her spit and polish was a woman who would someday make a man very happy, if she'd just give the guy a chance.

Too bad that guy wasn't him. But for now, at least, she was sticking around.

At the door, she looked back, the dark mask of her eyes soft with concern for Betty. Then the screen door slapped shut behind her and the boys.

Afternoon sun brightened the faded gray and white checkerboard linoleum floors. A siren sounded in the distance, growing closer.

He put his hand on Claude's shoulder. "She'll be all right." He'd seen lots worse during his stint in the Corps.

Claude took a deep breath. "Of course, she will."

Twenty-five minutes later, Beckett was standing on the front porch with Claude, the emergency medical team ready to transport Betty to the hospital for X-rays.

"They said I can ride with her to the hospital." Claude shifted uneasily. "Betty just took bread out of the oven when she fell. It's on the counter, still in the pans. Take a loaf home with you. I know she'd want you to."

"Thanks. I'll take care of it. Is there anything else you want us to do before we leave?"

Claude shook his head, then hesitated. The ambulance engines started. "No, but thanks."

Beckett watched the old man walk to the back of the emergency vehicle, his age and worries showing in the slump of his shoulders. After climbing in, he gave a brief wave before the doors closed. Seconds later, siren howling, the ambulance retreated up the drive, then raced toward town.

When he went back inside, Dakota was sitting at the dining room table with the kids. As was his new habit, Tucker lay at her feet.

JJ pulled a square of paper out of his back pocket and unfolded it. "I made you a picture. It's flowers."

Beckett leaned against the doorjamb, hoping not to disturb them.

"What a beautiful drawing." She smoothed the paper out on the table. "Thank you very much, JJ."

"Cousin Beckett said girls like flowers," Preston informed Dakota.

She glanced at him then. So, she hadn't missed that he'd been watching her with the boys. "He did, did he?"

"Yup," the boys said in unison, nodding energetically.

"Did he say how he knew this?"

He could practically see the wheels turning in her head. Dakota might not reason out that he'd had little time to date while he was in the Corps. What he did know was that his mom was delighted whenever her husband or son brought her flowers. Especially for no reason but to tell her they would love her till the end of the world.

"No, but he's probably given lots of girls flowers before," Preston decided.

My mother, Beckett mouthed at the lady arching her brows at him.

The dark brown of her eyes softened. Dakota turned back to the boys, reaching to pat their arms. "Well, he's right. Girls really like flowers. What do boys like?"

"Dogs!" JJ shouted, sliding out of his chair to wrap his arms around Tucker's neck.

Tucker wagged his tail. Relief made him breathe easier. The shepherd was going to make it.

"How amazing is that?" Dakota bent over to kiss Tucker's nose. "I love dogs too."

Who was this woman? What had she done with U.S. Marshal Dakota James?

Beckett concentrated on the boys, refusing to wish that kiss had been meant for him.

"Mr. Henley said we should take a loaf of bread home, but I don't think he'll mind if we have it here, as long as we clean up afterward."

"Will Mrs. Henley be okay?" Preston asked, both boys abandoning their play with Tucker to follow him into the kitchen.

Dakota came, too, and Beckett let out the breath he was holding. She went straight to the refrigerator to pull out butter and jam, placing the condiments on the counter close to the boys, along with butter knives and plates. The cutting knife for the bread was next to the loaves.

He would bet she had no idea how comfortable she looked moving around Betty's country kitchen. The four of them working together, waiting for the bread to toast, brought back memories of when he was a kid, waiting, mouth watering, while his mother cut the fresh bread she'd baked for him and his dad. It was proof that family wasn't just the one you'd been born into.

"Mrs. Henley will be fine. They're just checking her ankle to make sure it's not broken."

Dakota helped the boys butter their bread. She was good with kids and dogs. When she set her mind to a thing, she was all in. How could he not . . . appreciate that?

Beckett took a mental step back.

"This bread is so delicious." Dakota's tongue snaked out to catch the bit of jam left at the corner of her mouth.

Beckett's sexy-woman radar instantly sounded the alarm. He nearly reached out to wipe the sweet blob away himself, but managed to stop just in time. "It's even better than my mom's."

"Your mom makes bread?"

Taken capture by the surprised note in her voice—not a good thing, but he would dress himself down later—he cleared his throat. "I do too. She taught me when I was a kid about Preston's age."

"I would love to learn how to make bread this good."

"It's a date, then." The words were out before he could bite them back.

Dakota swiveled, all her relaxed movements evaporating. What a dope. He didn't mean date, date. He just meant—

What *did* he mean? Dakota had made it clear she wasn't the sticking-around kind. And he wasn't shopping for a girlfriend. Especially one who didn't have lifelong commitment on the brain.

Smirking, she gave as good as she got. "Sure. Okay. We can try a second date."

He frowned. "Second?"

"Yes. Even though we got off to a bad start, our kite-flying non-lesson was the first one." Humor tilted the corners of her mouth. The spark of laughter in her stunning eyes invited him to share in the laugh she was clearly having trouble keeping under wraps.

He gave in. "All right, second, then."

After cleaning up the mess they'd made, Beckett dropped the boys off at home and Dakota and Tucker where she'd left the Mustang. He'd just gotten to his room at the hotel when Claude called.

"How's Betty doing?"

"It's just a sprain, but her blood pressure is up a bit, so the doc wants to keep her overnight. I plan to stay with her."

They didn't have their truck at the hospital. "Do you need a ride home tomorrow?"

"That would be helpful, thank you." There was a tired sigh on the other end of the line, and then the silence stretched out for a long moment.

"Is there anything else I can do for you guys?"

Claude cleared his throat. "The thing is, I could use some help fixing up the barn. Can't pay much beyond room and board. I was hoping you'd hire on."

Beckett sat on the edge of the bed, facing the view of the ocean. It would get him out of the inn. "I have the dog."

"Tucker is more than welcome. There's plenty of room," Claude said gruffly.

An idea started to form in Beckett's mind. Dakota wasn't going to like it. "I can make that work. What time do you want me to pick you up?"

"Ten?" Relief flooded Claude's voice.

"Ten, it is." Beckett hung up and immediately started making plans.

Adopting Tucker had made him want to help other former military dogs. That had been the idea, after all, but then the idea became something else. Helping all veterans. He still wasn't sure how that might work out, but watching Dakota attempting to make her own transition to civilian life—

It gave him ideas. She gave him ideas.

There was just one thing. He would settle in Angel Point, busy with the veterans' project she'd inspired. Probably, before he found the right property and got the right permits, Dakota would be gone back to San Francisco.

Everything would go back to normal. For both of them.

Chapter Seven

WELL, THIS TRIP had turned out to be a bust.

She'd been so focused on talking Taylor out of her engagement, she hadn't given much thought to how or what she had to change so she wouldn't get fired when she went back to work.

What was it about people's drive to get married? She liked being on her own. Making her own decisions and not having to consider a partner's opinion. It saved a lot of trouble in the end.

It's a date, then.

Despite his weird idea of what constituted a date—not that she was much better—in another life, Beckett could be more than a friend. In all of this . . . trip to Angel Point . . . that was the most stunning revelation.

And, then there was Frank. He was due back any day. She definitely wanted to avoid that little family reunion. Without the excuse of saving her sister—what was she thinking . . . Dakota couldn't even save herself—what was she doing staying in Angel Point?

She'd been ordered to get her head together. She could

do that as easily in San Francisco as anywhere else. She didn't have to stay here with all these landmines hemming her in. Maybe she could talk Granger into letting her return to duty early. If that didn't work out, there was always Oahu, or she could just hang out and explore the city that was her new home. She'd never really gotten to know the places where she'd been stationed, only had gone from home to work and back again.

How pathetic was that?

More importantly though, the boss was right. She needed to straighten herself out. Not just to get back to work, but so she was back in control of her crazy emotions.

Dakota glanced at the suitcase standing against the wall. It was Friday. Not too late to pack her bag and point the Mustang south.

Decision made, she tossed the bag on the bed, open so she could throw in the few things she'd brought. Maybe it was the coward's way out, but she would call Taylor once she got back to her apartment. The kid could handle Frank's marriage to Camille without big sis getting in the way. Besides, it had the benefit of postponing Taylor's attempt to talk her out of leaving.

Tucker, asleep on his side near the door with his legs stretched out, whimpered. She squatted next to the shepherd and ran a comforting hand along his back. "Shhhh. It's okay, bud."

Sudden heavy knocking on the door woke the dog. He

instantly jumped to his feet. Grabbing him by the collar, Dakota answered the insistent summons.

She rolled her eyes. Beckett. Of course. He had the most unfortunate timing.

"Do you by chance cook?"

"Sure, if you count going to the deli or ordering in pizza. Why?" At least she didn't have to hunt him down to give him back his dog.

He followed her into the room, stopped, brows rising when he saw her opened suitcase. "Going somewhere?"

"Back to San Francisco. I'm glad you're here. You can take Tucker with you." She rolled up a pair of shorts and tucked them to the far side of the suitcase before going to the top bureau drawer and grabbing a handful of colorful tops.

With quicker reflexes than she would have given him credit for, Beckett snatched the shirts she'd stacked on the bed and stuck them back in the drawer.

"Hey! What are you doing?"

"I have a better idea." Before she could grab the shirts back, he closed the drawer with a firm push. "Claude has asked me to stay at his place and help him fix the barn. He's including room and board."

She stacked her fists on her hips. "What does that have to do with me?"

"With Betty's sprained ankle, she's going to need help around the house until she's feeling better."

Dakota narrowed her gaze. "No can do. It turns out, I'm

more handy with a gun than a fry pan."

His laugh was deep and rich. A funny happy dance started in her belly. "I'll bet you are, but the thing is . . . you have some free time. She likes you. So I think she'll let you give her a hand when she needs it. And Tucker will be there."

Clearly a bribe. One that stirred her suspicions.

"Hold your horses, mister. Why can't *you* play housemaid?" She glanced at the drawer where he'd stuffed her shirts back in. How hard would it be to make the man move aside?

"Very good question." He leaned against the drawer. "I already have a list of chores helping Claude repair the barn."

"Claude and Betty could hire someone to help with household chores."

"Claude suggested it. Betty won't hear of it. Visitors are okay, but she doesn't want strangers staying overnight in the house." He crossed his arms over his chest. His mouth shifted into a grin that only looked good on a Cheshire cat. "And it would give me a chance to give you that bread-making lesson."

"How long will Betty need me?"

Beckett's expression was unreadable. "Not sure, exactly."

Well, heck. Ramming him so she could get to her things would probably be like plowing into a brick wall. He was built like a lean linebacker. Impressive, but still annoying.

She huffed out an irritated breath, on principle. He was right. It wasn't like she really had anything else to do, except loiter in San Francisco or on a tropical beach.

On the other hand, if she stayed in Angel Point, trying something new might be helpful in recovering stable footing. Learning to make bread had its own appeal, but with Beckett as her instructor?

"When do you want me there?"

"How about now? I'll pack my bags. We can check out and sleep at the farmhouse tonight. It'll be an adventure."

Adventure? *Huh.*

Deep inside, an alarm was pinging a warning. Whether it was saying beware or welcome home, soldier, she wasn't sure. The Henley place was charming. And peaceful. A sanctuary. It would be a good place to regroup. Take some time to sort herself out.

And she liked Betty a lot. While she was there, even if it was for a short while, it might be a good time to try something else she'd never done—whatever that might be— besides making bread.

The one thing she wasn't signing up for was going gaga over Beckett Leland, though she suspected he might be worth the gaga.

She shot him a *you asked for it* smirk before waving him out of the way. "I'll meet you at the front desk."

He headed for the door, tossing over his shoulder, "Fifteen minutes."

She could pack up in less, but she wasn't going to tell him that. Rolling her eyes, she smiled after the door closed behind the tenacious man. Beckett was dangerous with a capital D. Guardrails were going up right this second. A girl who had her job to save had no business passing time with a hotshot former pilot who could possibly do a whole lot more than ring her bells.

Keeping that firmly in mind, Dakota grabbed her clothes and finished packing.

WHEN CLAUDE LET them into the house, a harried look deepened the lines on his aging face.

Uh-oh.

With a brief nod, he retreated. Beckett held the screen door open, waiting for her to go in first, a courtesy Dakota wished didn't impress her so much. But what the heck, it was nice.

In the living room, Betty was propped up on a brown colonial-style couch, leg sheltered on a bright blue pillow covered in bold red and orange flowers. Sun beamed through the windows, brightening the room, but Dakota didn't think Betty noticed. She wasn't a happy camper.

"Claude, this is silly. I don't want a nap, and I don't need help around the house."

"Now, sweetie, you know what the doctor said. You have to take it easy for a few days."

Dakota clamped down on a smile. She knew exactly how

the older woman felt. In fact, she would be throwing the same fit if someone she cared about coddled her unnecessarily.

But wasn't that what she was doing? Wallowing? She wasn't the only one Laney had deserted.

Betty uncrossed her arms and winced as she pushed herself so she sat up straighter. Dakota's irritation with herself melted immediately into sympathy.

"Maybe we should come back later," she suggested before Betty could continue her argument with her husband.

Startled, her hostess looked her way. "Oh, heavens. Of course not. You've just caught me at my worst."

Dakota parked her suitcase by a chair that matched the couch and sat on the floor next to the flushed woman. Tucker laid down next to her feet. "If that's all you've got, you have a long way to go to catch up to my worst."

It was definitely time to find some courage.

Betty's thin fingers covered her hand. "I find it hard to believe you're anything other than a very nice girl."

Dakota's eyes prickled. What a sweet thing to say. Not necessarily true but still, the sentiment was appreciated.

Beckett squatted behind her, the toe of his boot touching her foot, his hand resting lightly on her shoulder. His breath brushed across her neck. "Do you want me to take your bag up to your room?"

Holy moly.

"Please," she scraped out past the lump of—who the

heck knew what it was—in her throat. When he rose, she twisted to see that he was backing up, but his sharp gaze still rested on her flushed face. Needing her own distance, barely above a whisper, she reminded him, "Remember Cleopatra and Marc Anthony? They didn't make it."

He broke away first. Retrieving their bags, he turned to Claude. "Where do you want us?"

"There are two spare bedrooms upstairs. I'll show you."

"He likes you." Betty patted Dakota's hand.

"It's not like that. We're just friends." She watched the men leave the room before she turned back to Betty. "I should probably go up and unpack my bags. Do you want some water or something?"

Betty released her hand. Her face was remarkably unlined for her age, but her pale eyes held a wealth of plain tired. "No thanks, but would you mind helping me to my room? I think Claude's right. A nap might be the best thing."

"Of course." Dakota rose to her feet. She grabbed the crutches leaning against the wall.

It was a slow hobble to the bedroom on the first floor off the dining room. She helped Betty lay on top of the covers, then covered her with the quilt lying on the cedar chest at the foot of the bed. "Can I get you a book to read?"

She'd noticed several books on the end tables in the living room.

"Not right now." Betty closed her eyes. "Close the door,

would you, dear?"

Dakota softly closed the door, and thinking about the number of years between her and Betty's ages, made her way to the kitchen to put on a pot of coffee. When she got into her eighties, she didn't want to look back and see nothing but the same old struggles. Fighting with Frank. Watching Taylor grab the brass ring and being happy with Gabe. Coming home from her job—albeit a good job she loved—to the same empty attic apartment. Was that what she wanted?

No, but before she could move on, she had to figure out what she was moving on from, and why her emotions were all over the place. It was unsettling. And daunting. More impossible than hunting down and catching drug runners, which was her specialty.

Beckett, with Claude following, came into the kitchen. Crossing her arms over her chest, she backed to the window where Tucker lay on the floor. For sure, she didn't want Beckett Leland. The man, in his light-blue western shirt that brought out a playful look in his eyes, slim-fitting jeans, and well-worn cowboy boots, was every girl's dreamboat, but this was one mission she had to undertake on her own.

"Coffee smells good." Claude took down some mugs from the cupboard. "I'll take a cup to Betty. She loves her coffee."

"She asked me to help her to the bedroom so she could take a nap."

Claude, worry deepening the lines on his face, left the room muttering, "I'd better check on her."

Beckett leaned against the counter with the sound and smell of percolating coffee filling the kitchen.

"Claude and Betty have been together a long time. They'll be okay," she half said to herself, forgetting she wasn't alone until he handed her a cup of steaming coffee. "They're an exception. Just like your parents."

"They are definitely exceptional," he agreed. "Like Tarzan and Jane."

The man was stubborn. Compelling. Charming in his insistence that happy-ever-after was a real thing. He would make a strong safety net.

Hold up there, girl.

She didn't need a safety net. At eighteen years old she might have gone into the Marines to escape from home, but since she'd come to the marshals, she got why Frank and Taylor were so proud of the so-called family legacy. Even though Frank wasn't her father, she didn't want to be the first James to screw that up.

"What should we do for dinner? I noticed a grocery on the way here. They should have a deli."

Beckett shook his head, grinning as he explored several of the cupboards, including a floor-to-ceiling monster one that, it turned out, held all kinds of canned and dry goods. "Have you ever made spaghetti?"

She said dryly, "I know how to open a can."

It wasn't that she was totally helpless in the kitchen, she just enjoyed poking at the smug man who thought he knew her.

"How about we make spaghetti not from a can, then?"

"How about *you* make spaghetti not from a can?" she asked, tongue-in-cheek as she pushed away from the counter. "Which room am I in? I'll unpack while you're handling kitchen duty."

"Hold on there, Marshal James. First we make dinner, then we unpack. Unless you're too tired to be my sous chef." He winked and tossed her an apron he found hanging on a hook by the back door.

Beckett wanted challenge, did he? Well, she was his girl, then. Not *his girl*, but just his pain in the side.

Donning the apron, she wrapped the long ties from the back, around her middle, and tied them off in the front. "What's first?"

"You find a big pot to cook the pasta in. I'll get started on the sauce."

Dakota had never owned a place of her own; in fact, had always lived in base housing when she was in the military. In San Francisco, she was renting a small attic apartment. If she had a house like this, for once in her life, she'd consider giving up the nomadic lifestyle her career always demanded.

She found a pot for the pasta and filled it with water before placing it on the older gas stove. She lit the burner underneath. "What now?"

Beckett had hamburger sizzling in a deep frying pan. He handed her a package of long, thin noodles. "When the water starts to boil, break these in half and drop them in." He added salt and a little bit of oil to the water. "Can you cut up this onion?"

Taking the onion, knife, and cutting broad to the farthest counter from where Beckett was opening cans, she got to work.

A tea towel landed over her arm as the precisely cut onions disappeared into the meat pan. "You've done this before, haven't you?"

"It's not that I don't know how to cook, it's just not my favorite thing."

"What is your favorite thing?"

That was the million-dollar question, wasn't it? Shouldn't she know? "I like to hike." *And I like you.* "Is it crazy that I don't have a favorite thing?"

He took the towel from her, carefully wiping onion juice from her fingers. "That's not crazy at all. I'm sure a lot of people don't have a favorite thing they like to do."

Yeah, but why did one of them have to be her? "I should try some new things."

"Did you like being a Marine?" Releasing her, he retreated to his bubbling sauce, stirring once before replacing the lid.

"Mostly."

Without looking at her, which was a good thing since

the flush that had started while he was wiping off her fingers had climbed to her cheeks, he hunted in the cabinets over the stove. "Did you always want to be a Marine?"

It took a minute for her thoughts to come back from where they'd scattered. "What I wanted was to get as far away from home as I could."

Putting various spices on the counter, he stopped long enough to search her face. "It's none of my business, but why? Abusive home life?"

"No. At least, not the way you mean." In all fairness, she couldn't let Beckett think the worst of Frank, even if she did. Well, she didn't, entirely. She found a long-handled spoon and pushed the noodles around in the pot. "After Laney left, Frank and I didn't get along."

"I see."

He didn't, but that was okay. It was time she figured out a way to get over it. "How about you? Did *you* always want to be a Marine?"

"Not especially. My father was a Marine, and when I graduated from high school with good grades but no real plan for the future, he suggested the Naval Academy. So I applied, got in, and quickly found out I liked flying helicopters."

A flyboy. Given their different ranks, if they'd crossed paths, would she have wanted to date the fellow Marine? The Corps might have called that fraternization, but they weren't in the Marines now.

A date? Definitely not one of her favorite things.

"It sure smells good in here." Claude startled her from the doorway.

Dakota checked the boiling pasta.

Beckett pulled plates down from the cupboard. "I hope you and Betty like spaghetti."

"We like it fine, but I don't think Betty will have any. She says she's not hungry." Claude stuck his hands in the back pockets of his worn jeans.

Dakota looked around Betty's kitchen, with the light streaming in, white vintage cabinets, old-fashioned sink, faded checkerboard floor, and breathed in the charm the room exuded in spades. Tucker lay down and watched from a corner spot that gave the cautious dog an unobstructed view of the whole room.

Yup. Hiding out from her problems or letting someone else fight her battles for her wasn't going to work anymore. She'd always admired her sister for being the strong one. It was her turn to uncover the real Dakota James, whoever she might be, starting with—

She stepped away from Beckett. "I'll make her some pudding. Maybe she'll like some later."

Chapter Eight

WHEN BECKETT CAME downstairs early the next morning, the sun was just rising. The fresh aroma of coffee drew him toward the kitchen. He hadn't slept all that well. The women in the house had kept him awake most of the night, restless, and worried.

How could he make things better for them? Especially one tough-as-nails marshal.

You don't need to fix me. She hadn't said it out loud, but she may as well have.

And he didn't, but old habits were hard to break. He'd be better served, and so would she, if he got back to his own business. Dakota was heading back to the city. He was a card-carrying, certified country boy. Surprising as it was, Angel Point was becoming his town.

If he could have a relationship like Claude and Betty's, and a wife he didn't have to convince to stay around until they were well into their eighties, he'd consider himself to be one lucky dude.

Still, looking forward to seeing Dakota when he got to the kitchen, eyes closed in rapture, leaning against the counter and sighing over her first cup of fresh brew for the day, he was surprised to find Betty.

She pushed on her crutches, stretching for a mug in the cupboard over her head. Her fingertips just missed the mark. She wobbled. Beckett's breath stopped before he practically tripped over his own feet trying to reach the stubborn woman. "Let me get that for you, Betty."

"I almost had it," she huffed, easing back onto her crutches.

She sounded just a little twigged out, like his grandmother had when she was prevented from doing something she had her mind set on. His nana, like Betty, had been fiercely independent. His grandfather always said Beckett should never settle for anything less than a feisty woman. A feisty wife, he would say, was a special, rare find and would always make his life interesting.

If his grandparents were still alive, they would love Dakota.

If they didn't have two completely different ideas about love and marriage, he might consider something more than friendship with the surprising woman. Life with Dakota would always be an adventure. She, however, did not want to go on the same adventure.

Making sure Betty was steady on her feet, Beckett grabbed two cups. After fixing her coffee the way she liked it, he hovered while she hobbled to a seat at the dining room table.

"Where's Claude?"

"He slept in a chair by the bed so he wouldn't accidental-ly bump my ankle." She pinked up. Beckett hid a smile. "He was snoring when I woke up, so I snuck out so he could sleep a little longer."

"He's a lucky man, Miss Betty," Dakota said as she slid into a chair at the table. Looking like she was still half asleep, she propped her chin in her hand.

Bed hair stuck out at all angles. Eyelids drooped sleepily over dark eyes that normally didn't miss a trick. Beckett's pretty-lady radar pinged off the charts, along with regret that she was a Rhett and Scarlett girl, and he was an Aragorn and Arwen guy.

He went to the kitchen and came back with a mug full of dark roast he knew would wake Dakota up. He placed it in front of her.

Smoothing a clump of hair off her face, she glanced at him, gratitude softening the strong line of her jaw. "You're my hero."

On the other hand . . . but no. Dakota was still half asleep. She didn't mean he was her *hero*. She just loved her morning wake-up java. And he had Angel Point, Preston, JJ, and finding his own place. Not U.S. Marshal Dakota James.

Tucker padded into the room, gave a soft *woof*—the first one Beckett had heard from the shepherd since taking the dog on as a partner—and rested his nose on Dakota's lap.

"Gotta go, bud?"

The shepherd backed toward the kitchen and the back door. Dakota grabbed her coffee. "Okay . . . okay . . . I'm coming."

Dakota was too cute in her pastel-patterned pajama bottoms and matching sleeveless top as she followed the dog whose tail was wagging. He was beginning to believe, *she* was his hero, not the other way around.

Beckett turned to Betty instead. "Pancakes or waffles?"

"I can fix breakfast." She tried to stand.

"How about we take turns?" Hand on her shoulder, he gently held the older woman in place.

"I'm not an invalid. I can stand at the stove and cook a simple meal."

"I know you can," he said. "But I'm a bachelor, and I need to practice my cooking skills if I'm going to impress the women."

"Women definitely like men who cook," Dakota said with a smirk, leaning against the jamb.

He pretended innocence. His mom made no secret of the fact that she loved his dad's cooking. "Do they?"

"Sure." She shrugged. "Not me, of course, but lots of girls would appreciate your culinary efforts."

Amazing was the word that come to his mind. He kind of wished a long-distance relationship made sense, but it didn't.

Beckett winked at Betty. "Could be guys like women who cook, too."

"Which is probably why I'm still single," Dakota laughed.

He highly doubted that. But her laugh woke up parts that had only woken up one other time since meeting the lady.

Rewarding him with a saucy look, Dakota sauntered back to her seat. "Betty, when it's my turn tomorrow, would you mind showing me how to make French toast?"

"Of course, I wouldn't mind, dear."

Dakota's smirk sent his heartbeat into a perilous high dive before he could adjust his altitude. One thing was for certain. He would miss her when she left.

Beckett sobered. He was one lucky son of a gun. If he could pay that forward to Dakota, and Dakota to the next veteran, that would make a difference, wouldn't it?

"Okay, ladies, get ready for the best breakfast you've ever been served."

Fresh from the shower, Claude joined them before the last slice of bacon finished sizzling. He told stories about growing up in Angel Point.

When they were done eating, Beckett partly cleared the table. Dakota joined him in the kitchen, carrying the rest of the dishes, and put them in the sink to be rinsed.

"I thought we could go for a ride and look at property today. I found a couple online that might work. After, we can take a stroll down Warren Avenue. It's full of cute little shops you might like."

"That sounds like fun." She tilted her head a little, studying him as if she didn't believe all he wanted was to make sure she had a nice time while she was in Angel Point. That was what he wanted, right? "Tucker would like it too."

"Great. Let's finish up here. Then we'll head out."

Claude and Betty were still at the table, heads close together, holding hands. They were so dang cute together. Made him wish—

Dakota brushed his shoulder as she stopped with him to watch the couple. Did she see what he saw? "We're heading into town. Is there anything you need us to pick up while we're there?"

Claude shook his head, smiling at Betty. "It's Saturday, and on Saturdays, we always play a game of Scrabble. You kids go along and have fun."

Beckett drove. His Bronco had more room for Tucker than her Mustang. Dakota was quiet. Her phone pinged. Frowning at the screen, she turned it face down on her leg.

"Tell me about these properties we're going to see."

All right. It wasn't any of his business but—"Was that important? Do you want me to stop so you can have some privacy?"

She drummed her fingers on the back of the phone. "No. It's just Frank. He's on his way back from San Antonio and wants to get together sometime for dinner."

Whether she wanted it or not, Frank was her family. Like Stacy and the boys were his family. The exact relationship wasn't important. Only that the connection was there. On the other hand, she was entitled to choose who she called family.

A streak of white suddenly raced in front of the Bronco. Jerking the wheel to miss the animal, Beckett stomped on the brake. He was knocked back against his seat. Dakota slapped her hand on the dash to brace herself as the Bronco skid sideways across the asphalt. Tucker thumped against the back of her seat. They ended up on the wrong side of the road facing the opposite direction.

"You okay?" He did a quick survey. No blood, thank God. "Tucker?"

The shepherd whined softly.

Beckett twisted, reached as far as he could to run a hand over the shaking dog. No injuries that he could see. Another *thank you* echoed in his mind. "He's okay."

Dakota pushed hair dislodged from her scrunchy off her face. "I don't think you hit the animal."

"I don't think so, either." He searched the empty stretch of road in front of them and pointed at a dog across the street. "There."

A white shepherd limped back and forth. Dakota was closest. She eased out of the Bronco, keeping her movements slow and controlled. Letting Tucker out, she scratched his noggin. "Let's go make friends, bud."

Beckett beat them to the animal. "Stay back for a minute. I want to make sure she won't bite or fight with

Tucker."

"She?"

He nodded, totally focused on the stray until Tucker lay flat on his belly and barked softly as if telling the she-dog they were friendly humans. The other dog stopped pacing. Taking a chance, Beckett held out his hand for her to sniff.

"Be careful," said the woman who'd dashed across the road to make sure the stray wasn't hurt.

A tickle of warmth sprinted along Beckett's pulse. Maybe there was more to their friendship than he thought.

The dog took a cautious step toward his outstretched hand and sniffed. She took another step closer. Beckett knelt so he wasn't looming over the skittish animal. Finally, she shoved her nose into his hand.

"Hey, girl. Let's check you out." He gently examined the dog from nose to tail as he told Dakota, "No collar. I don't see any injuries."

Holding onto Tucker's collar, Dakota came closer. "She's still limping."

"The vet might know if anyone has lost their dog." Careful not to scare the animal or hurt her back leg, he lifted the female in his arms and started for the Bronco. "Can you get the door?"

Letting Tucker into the back seat first, she said, "Back up, Tuck."

When the shepherd stationed himself obediently on the other side of the vehicle, she climbed in next to him. "I'd better sit with her to make sure she isn't jostled too much."

"Easy, girl." Beckett gently put the dog on Dakota's lap. He covered the animal with the blanket he kept there. "While I drive, can you check for the nearest veterinarian on your phone?"

"My phone is in my bag in the front."

Sliding behind the wheel, Beckett glanced in the rearview mirror. Dakota was staring down at the dog in her lap. Retrieving her phone from the bag on the floor, he handed it to her over the seat. Turning the vehicle around, he headed for town.

"Head to Safe Harbor Animal Clinic. It's on East Monroe Street."

"I know right where it is. I've driven by."

The beauty of being in a small town was that it took less than ten minutes to get to the clinic. There was no one in the waiting room. He carried the dog to the counter. Hopefully, they didn't have to wait too long to see the veterinarian.

Dakota gave Tucker the hand signal to stay by the door. The shepherd dropped to his belly. Where had she learned that little trick?

The woman at reception was out of her seat and coming around the counter before he could speak. "What have we here?"

"She ran in front of us on the road. I didn't hit her, but she's limping. Is the vet in today?"

"I'm the vet. Dr. Channing Brown. Bring her in here."

Beckett glanced at Dakota and Tucker, who were both guarding the reception room as if they expected bad guys to burst through the door at any minute. "Can my friends come too?"

"Of course. This way."

Beckett followed the doc to a spacious room in the back.

"You can put her on the table." Dr. Brown positioned herself on the other side, her hands already reaching for the shaking dog. "It's okay, girl. No need to be afraid."

Keeping Tucker close, Dakota sat in one of the chairs along the wall.

Dr. Brown did a thorough exam, all the while talking gently with her patient. When she was done, she washed her hands. "You can help her to the floor now. She'll probably be more comfortable on her own four feet."

Beckett placed the dog on the floor. "What do you think, Doc?"

"There's no obvious injury. The most likely thing is that she has a bruise on the pad of that hind foot. I take it she's not yours?"

"No." Tucker came to stand next to the female. Beckett almost snorted out loud. His dog was a fast mover. "We were out by the Henley's when we found her."

"I know the place. Mr. and Mrs. Henley used to raise goats when I was a kid. They made the best soaps from goat milk." She smiled, drying her hands on a paper towel.

"Has anyone reported a missing dog?"

"Not that I'm aware of. She doesn't have a chip. No collar?" Beckett shook his head. Dr. Brown frowned. She reached down to pet both dogs. "Who is this handsome guy?"

"His name is Tucker. He's newly retired from the Marines."

She squatted in front of the dogs, holding her hands out to the animals. When Tucker edged forward, Doc Brown laughed and stood. "Well, looks like you've got your hands full."

Not as full as he hoped they would be.

"Let me take a picture of this little lady in case someone comes looking. Can you keep her until we find her family?"

Beckett didn't even have to think about it. "Not a problem."

"Good. I keep spare collars and leashes. Let me get you a set. It will save you from having to hunt them down in town."

"Thanks, Doc."

"Channing, please."

"All right, Channing. What do I owe you?"

She named a fee. Beckett handed over his credit card. After running the charge through, she gave him back his card and said, "Call me anytime."

Back in the Bronco, with both dogs settled in the back seat, Dakota said, "Dr. Brown seems nice. She likes you."

"Does she?" He backed onto the road.

"Sure. A girl can always tell. I'll bet she would love to be your vet for the dogs."

Perhaps, but Dr. Channing Brown didn't hold a candle to Marshal Dakota James.

Chapter Nine

*C*ALL ME CHANNING. Really?

Dakota snorted. It wasn't that she was jealous. How crazy would that be? Beckett was a good guy. Dr. Brown would be nuts not to notice. So why was she biting her nails over the veterinarian's flirtation?

"Dr. Brown is just being nice," Beckett said vaguely, his mind clearly elsewhere.

Dakota shook her head and grinned. Men. They couldn't see what was right in front of their faces when it came to women. She was pretty sure Channing wanted to be Lucy to Beckett's Ricky.

They finished the trip back to the Henley's farm in silence. Her phone pinged as he approached the drive that led to the farmhouse, a welcome interruption until, after digging her cell from her bag, she saw who the text had come from.

Dakota stared at the name on the screen. It was time to step back and reassess her situation, but it looked like she would have to deal with Frank at the same time.

"Your father, again?"

She nodded without comment.

"How long are you going to keep ignoring him?" Beckett asked quietly.

"For as long as I can," she muttered, staring at her hands. Taking a deep breath, she angled her chin. "I appreciate what you're trying to do. I do. But you don't have to fix me. This thing with Frank I have to figure out myself."

Beckett straightened his arms, pushing himself back into the seat. "My apologies. I know it's none of my—"

Regretting her words immediately, Dakota gripped the cell until her knuckles ached. "I'm sorry. I know you're just trying to help." *Calm down, James.* "Have you ever felt like you had to make a course change, and if you didn't, you would lose everything you'd spent your life building?"

As he slowed on the dirt road leading to the house, she felt the heat of Beckett's steady gaze. "Can't say I have."

"I have. I do."

"And this feeling has something to do with Frank?"

This time she didn't chastise him. Shifting so she could see the dogs, she faced Beckett at the same time. "When we were kids, no matter how much Taylor begged to get a dog, Frank wouldn't give in. He said he didn't have time to raise a mongrel and work and take care of his girls. Even when we were teenagers and could take care of ourselves, it wasn't allowed."

"I'm sorry," he said simply, reaching out to take her hand, dragging her stiff fingers away from her phone.

"Why did you have me take care of Tucker? Really?"

He kept his grip on her with one hand and the wheel with the other. "The two of you got along. And I trusted you."

He trusted her. Malcontent Dakota James. He trusted her. Why? She definitely didn't trust herself.

Sweet, but scary, too. He probably wanted her to trust him back but trusting others wasn't in Dakota's wheelhouse. Most recruits bonded with their fellow Marines, even made a family of sorts with other members of their units when they didn't have a stable civilian family to go home to. Looking back—didn't she have to in order to find a way forward?—her time in the Marines had just been a long string of days putting one boot in front of the other.

Talk about fixing things . . . her transfer to the so-called family business, as Frank liked to call the marshals, was supposed to fix her problems, but in San Francisco, her situation had only gotten worse.

The Bronco stopped in front of the farmhouse. She stayed absolutely still for the longest time, reluctant to shatter the understanding that had sprung up between them. It was absolutely mind-boggling—stupid, actually—that she could chase down the bad guys with the best of them but had no clue what to do to deal with her own issues.

As good as it felt to talk to someone about things she's always kept private, she couldn't just sit here with Beckett and wait for her best future to come to her. She'd read about that once: how to become the best version of herself. Maybe she shouldn't have dismissed the idea so quickly.

She faced Beckett. "I'm going to take that walk on Warren Avenue."

"All right. Let me see if Claude and Betty will watch the dogs while we're gone." He reached for the handle on the door.

"No. What I mean is, I want to go alone." The story of her life. He meant well, but she really needed to clear her mind without the distraction of Beckett. "I have to do some thinking. Will you keep an eye on Tucker while I'm gone?"

"Of course." He watched her closely, then frowned. "Are you sure you don't want company?"

"Very sure." Beckett might have a need to fix things, but he had kind eyes. Was one of those guys who would make it his life's work to make a girl's life better. It was sexy, be she couldn't take advantage of the offer. Not now. "Very sure."

"Okay." The tension left his arms and shoulders. He grinned. "Our new friend here needs a name. We can't just call her dog all the time."

Good point. From the back, Tucker stretched around the seat to lay his nose on her shoulder. "I won't be gone long, buddy."

Only long enough to clear the cobwebs and figure out what to do first. Pulling herself out of the quicksand she'd fallen into and moving forward was the only option she had left.

Dakota had no idea how to be happy the way Taylor was

happy, even before her sister met Gabe. Hoping to change that, she grabbed her bag.

When she looked in the rearview mirror all she saw was Beckett. He was flanked by both dogs as all three watched her spin away. She focused on the dirt road ahead of her. It seemed to take forever, but finally she reached the end of the drive. Before turning the Mustang toward town, she had to look one more time. Beckett and the dogs were no longer watching.

She found a parking spot on the south side of Warren Avenue, not an easy feat, since on Saturdays, Angel Point was the go-to place for tourists. At least, that's what the mayor said, according to Taylor.

A sidewalk sign just ahead advertised a secondhand shop a couple of stores down. She loved secondhand stores. How had she forgotten? Probably because the last time she'd been to one was with Laney.

Faith's Attic. Breaking free from childhood memories was a pain but suddenly it felt good to try. A bell over the door tinkled when she entered. Dakota paused, holding the door open as she took in vintage clothes, furniture, and odds and ends hidden in corners, begging her to explore. There was so much, if she had the time, it would take her days to dig around the strategically organized store. The whole place was a treasure trove.

A tall woman in a blue, vintage maxi dress that matched her eyes came forward from one of the corners. Long, blonde half ringlets hung down her back.

"I'm Faith Hathaway, and this is my attic. Can I help you?"

"Dakota James."

"Sheriff James's sister."

A laugh bubbled out. It felt good. "Does the whole town know I'm Taylor's sister?"

"Pretty much." Smiling, Faith tilted her head. "It's a small town."

Dakota let the door close. If there was ever a possibility that she would stay and make a permanent home in Angel Point—not that there was a chance of that—she could see the new Dakota James being friends with this woman. She followed Faith to a rack of vintage dresses.

"Are you looking for something specific?"

It had been a long time since she'd bought something so pretty for herself. "Not really. I think I'll just look around."

"Okay. Let me know if I can help."

The next hour, Dakota let her feet take her wherever they wanted and let go of the trouble occupying her mind. The only thing she couldn't let go of was the picture of Beckett and the dogs watching her leave the farmhouse.

Suddenly she was as far from the door as she could get and had backed herself into a corner. In more ways than one. She grabbed her cell from her bag and dialed her boss.

Granger picked up on the first ring. "U.S. Marshals. Granger."

Faith was dusting shelves on the opposite side of the store. What would it be like to have a job where the worst thing she had to worry about was keeping dust bunnies off her inventory?

"Deputy Marshal—"

Don't come back until you've got a grip. Granger's uncompromising order resurfaced with a vengeance.

"James," he acknowledged.

"Yes, sir. I'm, um, wondering if I can take an extra week off."

A chair creaked on the other end of the call as if Granger had rocked back to consider her request. "You sound good."

"I'm better," Dakota acknowledged. It was the truth. Not as good as brand new, but better, nonetheless.

"The case is moving slow. Take until July fifth."

He didn't sound annoyed, which was a good thing. "Thank you, sir."

"Take care of yourself, James." He hung up. That was Granger's MO, she'd discovered on her arrival at the San Francisco office. He wasn't one to waste much time or bother with prolonged conversation when a few words would do.

Exhaling a relieved sigh, Dakota put her phone away. While she was talking to Granger, a text came from Taylor that said simply, "Call me." Her sister could wait for a little while.

Continuing her roaming pattern, she stopped and stared

when she spotted a large, framed poster of the Eiffel Tower. Next to it were all kinds of Parisian paraphernalia, including paper plates and cups in their original wrap.

She snatched it all up, muttering, "You owe me one, kid."

Before she could head for the cash register, another framed poster, this one of Lucille Ball in her heyday, caught Dakota's eye. She started to pass by but then turned back. After Laney had abandoned them, she'd spent a lot of late nights in front of the television, with the sound turned down low, watching old *I Love Lucy* reruns. She figured Frank had to know, but he'd never said anything or gotten up to send her to bed.

On an impulse, she grabbed Lucy, too. At the counter, she stacked her stash.

Faith was unwrapping a box of porcelain figurines. She held up a miniature Tucker. At least what the shepherd must have looked like as a puppy. "Isn't he adorable?"

"Yes!" When Faith put the pup on the counter with the other figurines. Dakota added him to her pile. "I'll take it."

Faith laughed. "How long are you planning to stay in Angel Point?"

"Until July third."

Outside the sun was bright, warming Dakota on the inside. Putting her purchases in a bag decorated with her logo, Faith took Dakota's credit card. "You're not staying for the Fourth of July celebrations?"

"Can't. I have a long drive back to San Francisco."

"That's too bad. The fireworks here are fantastic."

Dakota liked fireworks. Maybe on the freeway heading south she would make a point of finding a high point where she could see some pyrotechnics.

Taking her bag of goodies, she started to leave, but then spun around. "It was nice to meet you."

"Same," Faith smiled. "Come back again before you leave."

Faith Hathaway didn't seem to have a care in the world. Dakota was more than a little envious.

"I will." She stepped out into the sunlight, juggling her packages and purse, looking for her keys.

"Kodie?"

She stopped abruptly. So, this was why Taylor wanted her to call. Dakota stared at Frank before blurting, "Stop calling me Kodie. What are you doing here?"

He stepped back, shoved his hands in his back pockets. "I saw your Mustang and remembered you were fond of secondhand stores when you were a little girl, so I thought I'd look inside on the off chance—"

A cloud moved in, obliterating the warm sunlight. In the distance, waves crashed into shore.

Dakota tightened her grip on her purchases. "Taylor said you were in San Antonio."

"I got back this morning. I would have returned sooner if I'd known you were here." His tone held disappointment.

Dakota didn't care. She had no desire to report her every move to the deputy marshal who purportedly was her father. Maneuvering around him, she took her acquisitions to the Mustang and shoved them in the back seat.

"Can we talk?" Frank asked from behind her. So, he hadn't gone away. "Dakota, let me buy you a coffee. Please?"

Huffing out a breath, she faced him. When she was a kid, she'd really, really wished, deep inside, he was her father. "Why? You talked enough when you came to South Carolina. You said I was a disappointment." Not that she'd ever made a conscious effort to make him a proud parent, but at MCAS Beaufort, he'd made her see just how empty her life had become. "I'm pretty sure that hasn't changed."

"It's not true. I was just trying to get through to you, but it was wrong to say those things." He pushed a hand through his cropped hair, then angled a shoulder toward Ginger's Coffeehouse across the street. "Just one coffee. I swear."

The half apology was unexpected. Taylor said Frank had changed. Maybe he had. Maybe he hadn't. She would see.

Dakota stepped off the curb, crossing midstreet to Ginger's. His footsteps followed, but it didn't matter. An iced coffee would go down pretty good right now, with or without Frank James demanding a conversation extricating him from whatever quasi-guilt he seemed to be carrying around.

She placed her drink order and claimed a table in the corner, a wall to her back, windows to one side, and open sight lines clear to the door. It was the same table she and Taylor had occupied when they'd come here after she'd first arrived in Angel Point.

Frank brought both coffees with him and took a seat so he could see the bulk of the coffeehouse, too. He might be retiring, but he definitely hadn't changed his ways, even if her sister said he had.

"How are you, Sis?" he asked, his expression tired and devoid of his usual stoic guard.

She shrugged. "Better than when I saw you last," she conceded. "I suppose you want me to thank you for *talking some sense into me*." The defiance bracing her shoulders deserted her. Grudgingly, she admitted the last thing she'd ever thought she would. "So, thanks. You made me reevaluate and make changes."

Looking uncomfortable, he shifted in his chair. "I have something to confess. You're not going to like it."

"I never take what you have to say seriously," she said with a liberal dose of snark. Heat flushed Dakota's face as her anger deflated. Okay, that was a little too in his face, even for her. She gripped her coffee with both hands. "I'm sorry. It's just that you bring out the worst—"

The man who was only too happy to let her know when she missed the mark was quiet for too long. For the first time in her life, it seemed he couldn't find the words to give her a scolding for her disrespect.

"Frank?"

"Kodie," he said. He didn't like being called by his given name by his daughters any more than she liked him using the short version of her name Taylor preferred. He leaned back in his seat before finally meeting her gaze. A deep frown pulled his brows together. "David Granger is a good friend of mine."

She hit the table with the palm of her hand. When the coffeehouse suddenly went silent, Dakota pushed her fist into her lap, remembering that it had been Granger who'd reached out to her with an inquiry about working on a new team he was putting together. Suddenly, it all made sense. The job offer. How surprisingly easy it had been to get the time off to come to Angel Point. Even that her new boss had made her leave sound like an order she couldn't ignore.

She reined in her anger and kept her voice low. "Did you get me the job in San Francisco?"

Frank started to reach for her, but she scooted back.

"No. You got the job on your own merits. David had already talked to you about his offer when he contacted me."

"So you told him about your reckless daughter?" Dakota tried to stop the words that sliced her in half, but just couldn't. "The one who couldn't go by the rules and never fit in?"

He shook his head, his eyes spilling his own hurt. "I told him he'd be lucky to get you. That you would be the best person for his team."

Swallowing hard, she wasn't sure she could believe him,

but Frank never lied. Except for the one thing.

She tried to hold it together. The words blundered out, anyway. "I heard you and Laney. The night before she left."

He stopped rotating the cup between his hands.

"You were fighting."

She couldn't look at him. After all this time, the punch to her heart still hurt too much. She should stop now. Not say another word. Before it was too late. She'd lived with the memory for so long. Why couldn't she just keep quiet and continue as she had before the incident in South Carolina, all buttoned-up, with her anger chained inside where it couldn't get out? That was the problem, though, wasn't it? The hurt wouldn't stay locked down anymore.

"You said you're not my real dad."

Closing his eyes, the strength that has always been Frank's best armor evaporated. She'd never thought to see the day when the steel that was his backbone and that made him a top deputy marshal cracked.

When his eyes opened, a troubled sheen of moisture tangled in his lashes. He reached for her hands. This time she couldn't retreat. "I can never make up for that. I wish so much that I could." A tear escaped down his face. "That night I was trying to get your mother to stay. I knew it would break your heart if she left without you." He squeezed her hands. "I may not have won the best dad award when you girls were growing up, but I just want you to know, and believe, I'm *your* father in all the ways that count."

Her throat closed off with crushing sadness. Frank handed her an envelope.

"What's this?"

"Adoption papers. I adopted you after your mom left."

She didn't want to believe him, except she did. Stubborn James's pride wouldn't let him do anything but tell the truth and take the hit on the chin. He dealt in facts, and the fact was, Laney didn't want her daughter. He had.

She swiped the moisture off her face.

"I don't know what to think," she said around the hard rock of emotion settling into her throat. She stared at their clasped hands.

"The reason I've been so hard on you and Taylor is because I failed to keep our family together," he confessed softly. Standing, he placed a gentle kiss on her head like he used to when she was a little, little girl. "I'm so sorry I took my disappointment in myself out on you and your sister. I hope you'll forgive me." He took a few steps toward the door, then turned back. "Taylor is having an impromptu pizza party this afternoon. She wants to talk about the bridal shower. I would love for you to be there. Camille would like to see you too. And I know Taylor wants you to come. Bring your friend, Beckett."

Beckett? How did he know—?

When the door closed behind Frank, unsettled and feeling like her whole world had shifted, she dug her phone out of her bag and punched the call button.

He picked up right away. "Leland."

"Do you know Deputy Marshal Frank James?" Dakota kept her voice calm by sheer force of will.

"Your dad? No. Why?"

"Can you meet me at Taylor's place?" She added, just so Beckett would know, "It's not a date."

"Okay." She didn't miss the amusement in his quick response. "I'll keep that in mind. When?"

"Half an hour?" That would give her some time to pull herself together after confessing her long-kept secret to Frank. "Bring Tucker and Lucy with you."

"Lucy?"

The curiosity in Beckett's voice, a true friend, made her feel better. She nodded. "Yeah. Lucy."

"I'll meet you there."

Friend?

It was foolish to think she had any other claim on Beckett. He was putting down roots in Angel Point. And she had no idea what she was doing except going back to save her job. But she was here now and had extra time on her hands to get her head together. She may as well take advantage of it and see if there wasn't more she could do for her *friend* than help him scout out property for his new business.

Chapter Ten

THERE WAS NO room left in the parking reserved for Taylor's restored Craftsman, so Beckett parked on the street across from Dakota's Mustang. He hadn't meant for her to get here before he arrived, but he hadn't counted on Betty asking for help to get flour and sugar from a high shelf in the pantry so she could make oatmeal cookies. Claude was still working in the barn, where they'd been all morning. How could he tell the sweet woman, who was the same age as his grandma, he had an engagement with a feisty marshal? A feisty marshal he'd promised to teach how to make bread.

He should have been on that a couple of days ago. A vision of the two of them in the kitchen, flour dusting their clothes, made him shake his head and smile. But then the warmth invading his chest faded. She still didn't trust him. That had been very clear when she'd gone off to town by herself. Dakota was one tough cookie, but something had to be very wrong for her to all of a sudden call him to reach out for help.

"Come on, kids. Gotta go help Dakota," he said to the dogs.

He'd just gotten the dogs out of the Bronco when movement in the Mustang's interior caught his attention. He crossed to the red beast, as Dakota liked to call the classic car, just in time to see her shove an envelope in her bag.

It wasn't the first time he'd seen her troubled, but it was the first time he had to fight with everything in him not to take her in his arms and whisper everything would be okay.

He opened her door. "What's wrong?"

She sucked in a ragged breath. Struggling to sling her purse over one shoulder, she shook her head. "Nothing."

Un-huh. Maybe here was his chance to earn that trust she held so tightly inside. He wasn't going to waste the opportunity.

Carefully, so he didn't put her into retreat—not that you could scare a fellow Marine—Beckett placed his hands on her shoulders and leaned close so she could see his sincerity. He cracked a crooked smile. "Doesn't look like nothing from here."

"I shouldn't have called you." She closed her eyes for the briefest of seconds and, seemingly without realizing what she was doing, leaned her forehead against his chest.

Beckett swallowed hard. "We're friends. Of course you should have called."

Friends. Right. He was starting to question if friendship was what he wanted from Dakota.

"Thanks for coming," she muttered and knelt to sling an arm around Tucker's neck before burying her nose in his fur.

With her other hand, she scratched Lucy's ear.

"No problem at all." Beckett didn't know what was going on, but he was going to find out. Whoever had gotten her this torn up was going to get a piece of his mind.

She gave the dogs a final pat, and without looking at him, ducked back into the Mustang. For a second he thought she might be leaving, but instead she emerged with a large picture of the Eiffel Tower, an arm full of packages, and a determined smile that trembled at the edges.

"Let me help you." He took the framed poster.

When they started up the walkway, Taylor and Gabe were framed in the large picture window. They were laughing. Dakota's steps slowed.

Shifting the picture, he placed a hand on the small of her back and wondered, "They look like they'll make it, don't they?"

"Maybe," she said softly, but it was high praise coming from the lady who didn't believe in such things. She stopped at the bottom step. "I ran into Frank today."

Beckett frowned. That would be enough to knock her off her stride. She'd been avoiding contact with the man for days.

He had to tread lightly here. "Everything okay?"

Dakota nodded, but her smile didn't reach her eyes. "I don't know. He wanted to apologize . . . and tell me apparently, he adopted me after Laney left."

He pulled her slightly into his side. Maybe he didn't have

to give Frank a piece of his mind after all. "Do you want me to come up with a good excuse to leave when you give me the signal?"

She went up one step, which put them at eye level. "You would do that?"

"You bet." Taylor would have to lock him up in her jail and throw away the key to keep him from completing this mission for Dakota.

"What excuse would you make?"

They climbed the rest of the steps onto the porch. He rang the bell and said, "Well, I could—"

Before he finished, Taylor swung open the door. "There you are. And you brought Beckett. Good." She stretched out her hand for the dogs to sniff. "You have a new dog."

"Taylor, meet Lucy. And you already know Tucker." He was glad to see Dakota's embattled expression ease as he introduced the dogs to her sister.

"I found some things for the shower."

Taylor's gaze flicked between them, not missing a thing, including that Dakota's semi-cheerful tone sounded forced. "Come inside. Frank and Camille are picking up the pizza."

Beckett followed the ladies, the dogs right behind them, as he put the poster of the Eiffel Tower in one of the chairs at the table so it faced the room and its occupants.

"Kodie, that's perfect," Taylor said, running her finger-tips over the picture.

Gabe put his arm around his fiancée's shoulders, pulling

her close. Even though Dakota was frowning at the two, sudden envy stabbed Beckett. In his estimation, they made the perfect couple. He should be so lucky someday.

Taylor took the bag Dakota carried. "What else have you got?"

"As ordered—plates, cups, some French trinkets. So that gets the shower details done, right?"

"I have to order the cake from Grant Reed—he's the new baker in town—but that should just about do it." Taylor gave Dakota a calculated look. "Speaking of Grant, he's single and a really nice guy. You should ask him out on a—"

Uh oh.

Taylor had a spark in her eyes that did not bode well for her sister. He'd seen that same look in his mother's eyes when she was up to her matchmaking shenanigans. That was his cue to get Dakota out of the hot seat.

Dakota swung both hands up like stop signs. "Don't say it!"

"—date."

"You said it," Dakota groaned.

He could have told her there was no stopping a matchmaker once they got it into their heads that the perfect match was the only way to save their single family member from a lonely, empty, bitter existence. Or so he'd been told more than once. His mother was no slouch in the matchmaking department.

"Gabe, don't you think Grant is the perfect guy for Dakota?"

Out of the corner of his eye, Beckett caught the doc's eye roll. "About as perfect as Beckett over there. Grant wouldn't make it past the appetizers."

For all her astute sheriff skills, Taylor was watching Dakota's reaction to her announcement, so she missed Gabe's meaning.

"But—"

Gabe put his arms around her. "Now, sweetie, let your sister pick her own dates."

Dakota shot him a *where's that excuse* look. That was his signal.

"Well, actually—"

Before he could finish, Frank came through the front door with Camille, both carrying a large pizza and the mouth-watering smell of pepperoni and pineapple. Frank seemed to brace himself when he saw Dakota. "Pizza's here, kids."

Taylor twisted out of Gabe's arms, saying under her breath, "Quick, put everything in the bedroom." Then, she blocked Frank and Camille's view.

Surprisingly, Dakota joined her sister while Gabe concealed the party decorations in a room down the hall. He figured Frank caught on, but Beckett wasn't sure how they pulled it off with Camille being none the wiser.

He offered additional distraction. "We can put those pizzas in the kitchen. How about I look for plates and napkins?"

Dakota slanted him a grateful look. One point to team Leland.

Gabe returned from the back of the duplex and whispered in Taylor's ear. It was too cute, for sure, the grin she gave the doc.

The James sisters could certainly hold their own. Beckett wouldn't mind being on the receiving end of one of Dakota's sassy grins.

They all sat at the table, the pizzas between them. Glasses of root beer were set out to wash the pies down.

"Since you can't get married at the Second Chance, have you decided on another place?" Taylor asked Camille, moving a slice of pizza to her plate.

Camille looked at Frank and shrugged. "We've talked about it and haven't come up with any ideas. I hate to get married at city hall, but we may have to."

"How about the Whale's Head Lighthouse?" Taylor suggested. "Russ Kingston—he's the mayor, Frank—was just telling me that the lighthouse and the park around it were bought this last spring. The new owner has recently opened up the grounds for special events."

Camille put her slice down. "Is that the one on the cliffs south of Angel Point?"

"Yes. I haven't been out to see it, but Russ says it's taken a lot of money to restore the property, which is why it's now available to rent. There was an article in the *Angel Point Gazette* that said the lighthouse is rated seventh out of the one hundred best places to kiss in Oregon. That should bring the new owners some business."

It was news to Beckett. Good information to have. If he was to, say, be interested in kissing, as a joint duty assignment, a certain former Marine . . .

Oh, man! He had to stop thinking of Dakota as a possible playmate. Brows arching, the playmate in question glanced his way.

Not yet, he mouthed as Taylor quizzed Frank and Camille some more. "When do you want to get married?"

"As soon as we can find a place." Eyes sparkling, Camille pushed thick red hair behind her ears, her whole attention focused on Frank. "We don't want to wait too long."

"We'll look into the lighthouse, then." Taylor narrowed her gaze on Dakota. "Do you realize you'll be the last James to get married?"

"I don't have a problem with that," Dakota said, flashing her sister a straight smile and him *the look*.

"But if you were dating—" Taylor took a long drink of her root beer, clearly only too happy to push back at her sister.

That was his cue. "Speaking of dates," he said, placing his napkin on the table. "We'd better get going. I promised to take Dakota for a walk on the beach."

"A walk on the beach? Are you guys dating?" Taylor pinned Dakota with a pointed stare. "Why didn't you tell me?"

Beckett reached across the table and took Dakota's hand. "That's my fault, Taylor. We wanted to keep it quiet for a little while. See if liking each other could work out. Especially since she lives in California and I'm planning to settle here. Isn't that right, Dakota?"

Her fingers twitched under his hand. She stammered, "Right. We want to go slow."

Beckett just wished she would smile so his story would be a little more convincing.

"We've got a bonfire to build and s'mores to make." He pulled Dakota out of her chair. The others, all except Frank—he had an amused sparkle in his eyes—looked stunned, as if watching a misfit play unfold. Beckett stopped long enough to ask, "Do you need help cleaning any of this up?"

Taylor shook her head. "No, we can take care of it."

"Great. See you later, then."

With the dogs jumping up to follow, they'd almost made their escape when Taylor stopped them with a calculated note in her voice. "Dakota, why don't you and Beckett check out Whale's Head and see if they can fit Frank and Camille's wedding into their calendar?"

Since Dakota didn't respond, he took it upon himself. "Sure. We'll check it out tomorrow and let you know."

Maybe it wasn't such a bad thing that he was an only child. Once he started the Bronco, he turned the vehicle toward the beach. They may as well keep to the fabrication of their "date."

"Why did you tell Taylor we'd check out the light-house?"

He shrugged. "It seemed the quickest way to get you out of there."

"You're probably right." After that, she stayed quiet until they reached the beach. It must have taken her that long to realize where they were going. "I appreciate the rescue back there, but you don't have to keep pretending you're taking me on a date."

He parked so they could watch the setting sun meet the skyline of ocean. The waves had calmed. Seagulls sailed gently overhead.

Thing was, he honestly didn't mind pretending. "I thought you'd like to see the sunset."

"Thanks." She leaned her head back against the headrest, gaze glued to the view.

Beckett let the soft silence between them take hold. Her eyelids slowly closed until he was sure she was asleep.

"Will you teach me to make bread tomorrow? But not because it's a date."

"Bread-making lessons first thing in the morning," he agreed. "Not a date."

Maybe he needed to think about taking her on a real date so he could get all this should they, shouldn't they, out of his system.

THE NEXT MORNING, despite the five o'clock hour, Dakota beat him down to the kitchen. The door to Claude and Betty's room was still closed.

Taking the cup of coffee she offered, he quietly said, "You don't have to go to the lighthouse today. If you want, I can check it out for Taylor."

"I'll go. Besides, Betty is looking forward to the picnic." They'd decided to take a picnic lunch. "Bread lesson first, though."

"Okay, bread it is. We'll need warm water, yeast, brown sugar, salt, eggs, and flour," he recited from memory.

Dakota gathered the ingredients, except water, and put them on the counter. "You said your mom taught you to make bread? That seems like an awfully simple recipe. Where did she get it? You're sure it makes good bread?"

He laughed at her rapid-fire questions. "The best. And it's super easy. Mom got the recipe when she lived in England after my dad was stationed there. She had a friend who had a friend . . . you know how that goes in military families."

"Huh." He could tell by her expression she didn't know. That was a surprise but then, maybe not. "So where do we begin?"

He found a bowl large enough to hold the ingredients as he turned them into dough. How in the world had she got through military life without making the kind of family that came naturally to personnel so often stationed away from home?

He turned on the hot water, showing her how to test the temperature with her wrist, just as his mom had taught him, then added ingredients in the correct order.

She bent over his arm, barely touching as she watched closely. She was close enough he could smell the flowery shampoo she used.

"Grab that towel, spread it out, and dump about half a cup of flour on it."

Dakota did as he instructed, her movement economical and precise. "Like this?"

"Yup. That's perfect."

So is she.

Well, crap. It was thoughts like that one that were going to get him in trouble.

"Here, I'll show you how to knead the dough." He pushed on the dough, folded the glob, trapping the excess flour to give the dough ball more consistency. He stepped out of the way. "Your turn."

When she struggled a bit with the unfamiliar moves he put his arms around her from behind. "May I?"

She nodded. He breathed in her scent and coached her on the fine art of kneading bread, though how he kept his mind on the task was beyond Beckett. He finally took a step back before he could give in to another impulse, like stealing a quick kiss.

"Now what?" She sounded breathless. Thank God it wasn't just him.

Enjoying the sweet smell of a summer morning, baking bread and taking a breakfast break on the front porch swing? Probably not.

"We put the dough back in the bowl. Cover it with a towel. And set it in the sun on the counter here to rise."

"How long?"

"An hour, I'd say?"

"I'm going to check out the barn while we're waiting." As if reading his thoughts, Dakota backed toward the door leading to the back porch. Tucker and Lucy jumped up to go with her.

"How about breakfast?"

"Not hungry," she tossed over her shoulder as the screen door closed behind them.

Beckett frowned. So, no morning swing. No pretending they were a couple with nothing better to do than slather butter on the bread they'd just made. Together. Like a couple who had the secret to making their relationship work for the long haul.

Clearly, that wasn't one of the new things Dakota wanted to try. Lesson learned. Stick to earning her trust. If he could do that, he will have accomplished quite a feat.

Chapter Eleven

DAKOTA WAS BREATHLESS by the time she reached the sanctuary of the barn. Just inside the door where the rays of the sun couldn't reach and she wouldn't be seen from the house, she bent over, hands on her knees, and breathed in and out, deep breaths. Eventually her pulse slowed enough that the rush of her blood was no longer all she could hear.

For Pete's sake. It was just her first time making bread, not inventing a cure for the criminal mind. Just because kneading dough with a guy—a really good-looking, sweet guy, his strong arms caging her in—had been the most excitement she'd had in ages, didn't mean she had to get lost in the moment. She had more strength than that, didn't she?

Didn't matter. It was appealing to think about spending more time in the kitchen with Beckett's arms wrapped around her, even hypothetically. Dakota was tired of having no one to share her morning coffee with. No special person to take her on evening walks when their jobs permitted. No one to make bread with on a Sunday morning. No one to go on a field trip with, to explore property for dogs whose lives were moving on from military duty.

Just like her. Beckett hadn't only shown her how to make bread, he'd shown her how much she didn't want to go back to a life filled only with duty. Straightening, she sucked in one last, steadying breath and wandered deeper into the barn, where soft morning shadows offered comfort and maybe some clarity.

Over the years, she'd turned her back on Frank. And Taylor, really. Even though she'd let her sister hang out around the rough edges of her so-called independence. Independence, *pfft*. She'd just been too afraid to let anyone get too close. Afraid she would lose them like she'd lost Laney and Frank.

Dakota didn't want to be that girl, and she definitely didn't want that life anymore.

Windows were placed here and there along the length of the barn, which was as neat as a little-used barn could be. Kind of like Marshal Dakota James. All shined up on the outside. Tired and mostly neglected on the inside.

Why hadn't Frank told anyone about the incident on the base at Beaufort and how he'd found her three sheets to the wind? As far as she could tell, he hadn't mentioned it to Taylor or Granger. If she'd known, Taylor wouldn't hesitate to rake big sister over the coals. More than once. Granger would have withdrawn his job offer. He wouldn't want a loose cannon on his SOG unit, even if he was good friends with Frank and doing him a favor by hiring Frank's off-the-rails daughter. That she was doing her best to find her way back wouldn't have mattered.

Then there was the man who loved dogs and could make bread. Dakota sobered. He belonged in Angel Point. She didn't. The last she'd checked, there wasn't a marshal's office in the small town.

All she knew was that she couldn't continue to blow up her career, because being a special ops was the one thing she knew how to do and do well. And she liked the work.

In the far corner of the barn, she found a stack of crates and took a seat on the nearest box. All the skills and strengths that made her a good Marine and marshal, like being hyper-focused, keeping her emotions in check, her objectivity on point, and never giving up on a pursuit no matter what, they were also the same skills she'd used all these years to keep herself out of reach. It was a hard truth to swallow.

Beckett found her still sitting here. He crossed the empty space and sat next to her, his shoulder brushing hers. "So, what's up?"

Frank wasn't really the villain of the story she'd always made him out to be. That role was hers.

She stared at her hands, fingers laced, as she leaned toward Beckett. What was it about him that scrambled her thoughts?

"Just had some thinking to do. Where are the dogs?"

"With Betty." He got up and started investigating the stack of crates behind them. "Did I ever tell you why I really left the Corps?"

She shook her head. He'd said he decided not to reenlist. She said the same thing about her transfer from the Marines to the marshals. Mostly she didn't want to talk about the real reason, so it'd been easy to let Beckett keep his reasons private when he said his streak of luck had run out.

"I did three tours in Afghanistan. My team called me 'Lucky Dog' because I could fly, even in the worst firestorms. I never went down and never lost a teammate." He moved one of the boxes so he could inspect the one behind.

Dakota stood, too, stepping aside so she could watch this man who—it was scary to say—could, perhaps, be something more. If she could figure out the logistics of what a real relationship with a man like him looked like. Even a short one. She only had a little over two more weeks in Angel Point to figure it out.

"That last flight, when my Viper went down—"

"Your luck ran out," she finished for him. She could feel his pain. Been there, done that, as far as holding on to her luck was concerned.

He nodded. "We made it out, but I had a broken leg." He swiveled to face her. "That's how I hooked up with Tucker. I went home to recuperate and got there at the same time my parents were adopting him."

"And then you both came here?"

Beckett sat on one of the boxes. "Yes. While I was home, I decided not to reenlist. I haven't flown since getting out."

Dakota came to stand beside him. She wanted to brush shoulders like he had with her, to show . . . she didn't know what, but at least her support. "I got out because I couldn't go into another house to find a fellow soldier out of his mind, his family locked in the bathroom."

And because finding the kids in that bathroom, hands covering their ears, took her right back to that night when she'd heard Frank and Laney fighting. When she'd realized neither one of them wanted her, she'd locked herself in the bathroom and cried her heart out. Later, when Frank had knocked on the door and asked if she was okay, she'd wiped the tears from her cheeks and told him she was fine. From that day on, that was what she told everyone.

Beckett scrubbed his face. "We're quite a pair, aren't we?"

Pair? "I guess. You know you have to fly again, right?"

He studied her quietly. "Is that why you signed up for the SOG unit? So you don't have to face the fear that domestic situations can crop up anytime, anywhere on your watch? Trust me, they will."

"I wish it were that simple." She gave him the point and sighed heavily. "You're right, of course." Dakota stared at the crates. "So what's in all these boxes?"

"Soap-making equipment, I'm guessing." He glanced over his shoulder. "Remember, Channing said Claude and Betty used to make soap."

Channing.

She gulped in a shaky breath. "Is it time to check on the bread?"

"Probably."

Dakota was acutely aware of Beckett's presence at her back as she headed for the house. When they got close to the barn door, she came to a halt and faced him. "Thanks for coming to check on me. I know I can be a pain, and I'm not good at saying the right words, but I want you to know I appreciate the effort."

It was the right thing to say, because the tension that had taken over Beckett's usual good nature while they talked dispersed. "Happy to help."

Feeling lighter for telling him about Frank and what happened in South Carolina, she walked side by side with him into the mid-morning sunshine.

"We should ask Betty about the equipment in the barn. Maybe she'll teach us how to make soap." He stuck his hands in his pockets.

Dakota snorted. "Maybe she'll teach *you* how to make soap."

"I'll bet you'd be good with the equipment."

"What makes you think that?" she asked.

He stopped, one booted foot on the first porch step. "Look how easily you change a tire. And you probably do most of the maintenance on your Mustang."

He would be right about that. She didn't trust anyone else to take care of her baby the way she did.

"Not the same skill set, Leland," she said cheekily, scooting around him to the back door.

She glanced over her shoulder. The smile on his good-looking face did more to lift her out of her doldrums than anything had in a long time.

The dogs met her as she entered the kitchen. Betty was cooking eggs and bacon at the stove. Claude hovered under the guise of supervising.

The idea of staying here with Beckett and the dogs, with the Henleys as neighbors was too tempting. It made her feel like she was part of something bigger than herself for the first time since she'd graduated from boot camp.

She would miss these people and all of this when she went back to San Francisco, which only meant she'd better enjoy her time in Angel Point.

"Looks like you can put that dough in bread pans and let it rise one more time before you put it in the oven," Betty said as she turned over the bacon. "Breakfast will be ready by the time you're done."

Dakota wished she'd had a grandma like Betty. To teach her things. Keep her on the straight and narrow. Frank had done his best, but couldn't keep her out of trouble. That was her fault too.

After washing her hands, she followed Beckett's instructions to the letter. Punched the dough in the bowl down. Cut it in half. Formed each one into a mini loaf and carefully placed them in greased glass pans.

"Good job." At her elbow, he praised her efforts, causing a flutter in her stomach as he moved the pans to sit in the warmth of the sun before covering them with a light tea towel.

She shouldn't feel like she'd conquered Mauna Kea in Hawaii—something that was definitely on her bucket list—but she did.

They were seated at the table eating breakfast when she remembered the crates in the barn. "Dr. Channing Brown, the veterinarian in town, mentioned you guys used to have a soap-making business?"

"Yup, what's left of Betty's soap-making equipment is in the barn," Claude said, pushing back his empty plate.

So, Beckett was right. Dakota leaned forward on her forearms. "What happened to your business?"

"We started Henley's Soap Company on a whim, thinking we might make a little extra retirement money." Betty wrapped her fingers around her teacup. "But there wasn't a market for our soap in Angel Point. After a while we were spending more than we were making, so we had to close the company."

"Soap made from goat's milk. That's a cool idea." Finished with her breakfast, Dakota stacked the empty plates.

"We thought so too." Betty sipped her tea. "We were sad to have to close up shop."

Making soap sounded like something new and fun, if she ever had the opportunity or time. Even Beckett seemed interested as he listened intently.

"When was that?"

"About six years ago. I remember because I'd just cele-brated my eightieth birthday."

The lady still had her spunk. Dakota admired Betty for that, having lost her own spunk in South Carolina.

Beckett drummed his fingers on the table. "I need to come up with a company name for my business. Any ideas?"

"How about Leland's Therapeutic Canines?" Claude suggested.

Dakota picked up the stack of plates. Before she got all the way into the kitchen, she leaned back into the dining room. "How about Leland and Company?"

"I like it," Betty concurred.

"How about Leland and Company Farm?" Beckett sug-gested.

"I think you've got a winner there, son." Claude followed Dakota with the leftover food.

"Of course, I still have to find a place to build the busi-ness," Beckett said ruefully.

Dakota took her armful to the sink, a light spring in her step. It *was* a good name for Beckett and his dogs. "Tucker, move out of the way, bud."

"I was talking to Harry Baldwin, my neighbor, this morning and he's putting his place up for sale. He and the missus are moving to Arizona to be near the kids."

"Where's his place?" Beckett asked, his eyes lighting with

interest.

"Right next door. There's a house, outbuildings, twenty acres, and a creek out back." Claude put the orange juice and leftovers in the fridge. "Harry and Katherine are making a quick trip to Arizona today to sign papers on their new house down there. If you want to take a look, I can see if I can get a key."

"That would be great, Claude. Appreciate it. I'd love to look at it." Beckett lifted the towel from the rising bread. "The bread looks like it's ready to go in the oven. While that's baking, will you show me the equipment in the barn? Maybe you could sell it for some extra cash."

Claude shook his head. "We tried when we closed the business. Nobody was interested."

"While you gentlemen are playing in the barn, Dakota and I will get the picnic ready," Betty said, pulling sandwich makings out of the fridge. She still limped, but wanted nothing to do with the crutches. More often than not, she left them leaning against a wall.

The men went out the back door, taking the dogs with them. It felt too much like being part of a normal family, which was kind of crazy. The unfortunate thing was, she was very tempted to pretend it was true for the remaining time that she was in Angel Point.

She turned back to the older woman who was humming as she made the sandwiches. "Should you be standing on your ankle this much?"

"I'm fine. My ankle's getting better." Betty packaged the finished sandwiches in clear wrap.

Dakota figured there wasn't much she could say that would slow Betty down. She tried, anyway. "You should at least be careful not to reinjure it."

"Yes, ma'am." Betty's eyes twinkled. "You sound like my mother when I was a young girl. She was constantly after me to slow down."

Dakota had heard the same thing. "It's probably good advice."

"When are you going back to San Francisco?" Betty asked with a mischievous note in her voice.

Dakota dug around in the fridge until she came up with grapes and blueberries. "Two weeks, maybe?"

"Do you have to go?"

It was sweet that Betty sounded a little disappointed, but sooner or later she *did* have to leave. "My work is there."

"That's too bad. I think you'd love living in Angel Point." Betty pointed to the pantry. "On the bottom shelf is a picnic basket."

Dakota couldn't remember the last time when she'd actually loved living anywhere.

By the time the men came back, the bread was out of the oven and cooling on a rack. The wicker basket was packed. After loading up the dogs, Beckett drove.

"There's the sign." She pointed at a road to the right, angling toward the coastline. "Looks like we turn here."

The drive up to the lighthouse was breathtaking. A circular tower rose white and tall against a blue sky. The lens at the top glinted like a large jewel in the sunlight. There was an attached keeper's dwelling. Both were shingled in red tiles. Ironwork and shutters were black. Seagulls screeched as they circled overhead and dove over the cliffs toward the water.

It was a spectacular vista but reminded Dakota, taking a nosedive into the unknown was exactly what she was doing. When she got out of the Bronco with the others, a pushy wind nudged her from behind, flipping her hair in her face. Beckett put the dogs on their leashes. "This is so lovely," Betty said, leaning into Claude. He'd grabbed he basket.

Agreeing with Betty, it was a minute before Dakota realized the vehicle parking next to them was Taylor's truck.

"Hey, Sis."

"What are you doing here?" Dakota hung back while the others moved toward the lighthouse.

Taylor threw an arm around her shoulders. "I saw you turn off the road and figured it wasn't fair to make you check out the lighthouse by yourself."

"You were pretty bossy, but as you can see, I didn't come alone."

"I noticed that." Taylor winked and linked their arms. "Let's go check this place out for Frank."

Beckett had stopped and was waiting for them to catch up. Dakota heated up at his protectiveness. Maybe he was just waiting for Tucker? She waved him on. His brows rose, but he took the hint.

"Beckett's a cute guy."

Dakota laughed. "Will you cut it out? He's just a friend."

"If you say so. The lighthouse owner's name is Sidney Parker. I called earlier to let her know you'd be stopping by. That must be her there."

They walked toward a woman who seemed too young to be a lighthouse keeper, although there was no real reason to expect someone older. After introductions, Sidney gave them the two-cent tour and a thorough history of the lighthouse. Dakota loved it, but Taylor loved it more. "I'll tell Dad about it and Camille will probably get in touch with you about setting a date."

Dad.

Sidney held out her hand to Taylor. "We're just getting started with hosting weddings, so our calendar is pretty open."

They shook hands. Taylor hugged Dakota before heading for her truck. "I have to get back to work. I'll let you know what Frank and Camille decide."

"Hang on a minute."

Taylor stopped. "What is it?"

Dakota sucked in air, not sure where to begin. Finally she just blurted, "Frank isn't my father."

"Maybe not your biological father, but he is your dad." Taylor took her hand and squeezed.

Dakota bit her lip to hold back the moisture flooding her eyes. "You know?"

"I was awake. I heard their fight the night before Laney left, too."

"But you never said anything." With the back of her free hand, Dakota brushed the tear that managed to escape.

Taylor shrugged. "I figured if you wanted to talk about it, you would. Kodie, it never made any difference to me, or to Frank, really. You're my sister. Nothing will ever change that."

"Well, what you don't know is that he adopted me after Laney left."

"He did? Good."

Dakota grabbed Taylor and held on tight until her sister tickled her ribs like when they were kids. She laughed and let the kid go. "Get to work, lazybones."

Taylor inclined her head toward Beckett. "You get to work too." With a chuckle, she took off toward her truck.

Beckett walked toward her, minus his usual canine entourage.

"Hey!" She spun back to Taylor.

Her sister stopped. "What?"

"I thought you were batting for team Grant."

Taylor raised both hands in apparent surrender, but a big grin spread across her face. "I don't think it hurts to have options."

"Ha, ha," Dakota said, but Taylor was already climbing

into her truck.

"Everything okay?"

Dakota swung to face the man at her back. With no more thought than it took to put on her badge each morning, she pushed up to her toes and kissed Beckett. Squarely. On. The. Mouth. And she lingered until she dropped back on her heels.

After a surprised second, he kissed her back. Dakota liked it. Dove in with every turned-on cell in her body.

"What was that for?" His voice was deep, gravelly, and made her want to curl her toes in delight and go in for a second helping.

"To say thank you." Maybe that wasn't all the kiss was about, but it was enough for now.

She almost floated on air on their way back to the lighthouse. She would go back to San Francisco glad to prove to Granger that she was a new person. But before she did, she would give Angel Point a try and get to know the folks who called the charming town home. That included Beckett Leland.

Chapter Twelve

BY TUESDAY, BECKETT had spent way too much time going over and over a kiss—according to Dakota—that she'd meant to be a simple thank you. It hadn't felt simple.

The sixth sense that had protected him every time he flew a mission pinged a warning. Just because he'd kissed Dakota back and would happily volunteer for a second engagement did not mean he planned to lose his head. Better to keep his distance than do that.

With stiff strokes, he raked the area around the chicken coop into a heap of shriveled leaves and pine needles. Scooping the pile into a waiting wheelbarrow, he added scattered tree branches as he waited for Stacy to drop off Preston and JJ for the morning. He'd volunteered to watch them while their grandma ran errands.

It wasn't a serious kiss, and he had a long list of things to accomplish without adding an impossible attraction for Dakota James that could not lead anywhere. Unless . . . but no.

She had her eyes focused on returning to San Francisco, not loitering around Angel Point helping him set up a place for his dogs, and maybe, if he could work out the details, a village for veterans transitioning to civilian life, the same as his dogs. It was an idea that had taken hold when he read an article in *The Oregonian* that morning about a village in Clackamas County.

He looked over the fence at the Baldwins' property. In the distance, he could see a single-story farmhouse and large barn, not that different than the Henleys', but otherwise, there wasn't much to see. There was a connection there. He just had to figure out how the puzzle pieces fit together.

The only outlier was Dakota. Would she agree to be his partner in the venture? As much as their kiss had taken over his imagination, so had establishing the village.

He'd never been a one-night or one-week stand kind of guy. If he fell hard for a girl, he wanted what Dakota didn't believe in. Forever.

She came around the corner of the barn with Betty. The dogs ambled close behind and dropped to the ground nearby. "Look what I did."

He and Claude had spent all day yesterday unpacking and setting up the equipment in the barn, so Betty could show Dakota how to make soap. There wasn't much to unpack, but it had made her happy and that was all that counted.

"Let's see." He put aside the rake and took the bar she held out. "It smells like—"

"Lavender!" she said, almost bouncing.

He laughed. No matter how hard he tried, she was just too hard to resist. It *was* quite an accomplishment for a lady whose only hobby seemed to be catching the bad guys and protecting the innocent.

He returned the soap. She smelled it, rubbed her thumb across the surface. "When you get your place, you should buy goats. I've been doing some research and goat milk is one of the best things for your skin."

"Can't."

Dakota would fit right in if she ever decided to leave the marshals and move to Angel Point.

Her brows came together in an unwavering line. "Why not?"

"Can't take care of them. My priority is the dogs," he reminded her gently. "They're going to take all my time and attention."

Betty's gaze shifted between them. He had a feeling he didn't want to know what Mrs. Henley was thinking.

Dakota's exuberance dimmed. "Sure. That makes sense." She took a step back. "I'll go clean up the equipment."

Dang it. He wished he could get her the goats. He didn't like being the one to burst her happy bubble. From what she'd told him, she'd had enough of that when she was a kid.

Just then Preston and JJ ran around the corner of the house. They stopped to pet the dogs. "Cousin Beckett! We're here."

"I can see that." Their energy was contagious. He

laughed. "You boys want to help me fix up this chicken coop?"

"Yes! Yes!" they shouted, jumping to their feet. JJ did a little happy dance. "Then we can get chickens! What should we do?"

"Take this wheelbarrow over to that pile over there and dump it."

The boys wrestled the wheelbarrow between them, tipping it over before they got to the pile.

"You know, Preston and JJ could take care of the goats," Betty observed with a small smile as she watched their antics. "The animals aren't much work, and the responsibility would be good for the boys."

Beckett moved to stand by her as they both watched the kids kick the small pile toward the larger one. "Possibly, but they'll have chickens to take care of. Are you sure you want to get chickens?"

"Absolutely. It will save us having to get eggs at the grocery." She turned to the barn. "I'd better go help Dakota clean up."

Beckett spoke before he thought the ramifications through. "Can you ask if she'd like to help us with the chicken coop?"

If keeping his distance was the plan, inviting her to help with a chicken house and still unformed plan for vets wasn't the way to stay out of the minefield.

Eyes squinting with a twinkle, Betty nodded. "I'll ask

her."

Beckett watched until she disappeared around the corner. She was moving a little slow today. When she went out of sight, he gave JJ something more constructive to do than make a mess of the debris he'd already raked up once.

He took the rake to the boy. "JJ, why don't you use this to get all those leaves in the big pile?"

He showed JJ how. His exuberance reminded Beckett of Dakota and her excitement over the goats. What was he thinking? No goats. Nowhere to put them, even temporarily until he decided on and paid for the property. No one to take care of them even when he did.

He squatted next to Preston. "What are you doing, buddy?"

"Watching that hummingbird." All the kid's happy abandonment from earlier was missing. "We have feeders on the back porch at home." Preston paused, but eventually continued. "My dad loved them."

This was the first time Preston had opened up to him about Jason.

"I didn't know hummingbirds lived in Angel Point," Beckett said carefully.

The kid picked up a small pebble and tossed it. "I miss him."

"Me too." He rested his arm across Preston's shoulders. "Your dad would love that we are fixing the chicken house. If he were here, he'd be the first one to help. He loved hammering things."

Preston looked up. "Mom says he liked to fix things."

Nine years old was too young to shoulder the grief that came with losing a parent. Even though it'd been more than a year, the loss of their dad would never really go away. "Let's check to see if we need to do repairs first. Then we'll paint."

They stood together. JJ had done a pretty decent job of getting all the debris into one pile.

It was a good reminder. Even though he had a business to get off the ground, he had people counting on him. These boys needed a guy in their lives to give them a dad's advice and steer them in the right direction. That was a job he was willing to take on.

He felt eyes on him. When he looked over his shoulder, he found Betty and Dakota crossing the yard to the house. Dakota took measured steps to accommodate the older lady's slower gait, but she was watching him with the boys.

From this distance, he couldn't tell what she was thinking, but he did know one thing. He couldn't let himself get sidetracked with her problems or that thank-you kiss. Except that was already a lost cause. He might have a list of his own to deal with, but she was a veteran. And helping veterans was looking to be his end game.

You are so in over your head, dude.

The ladies disappeared into the house. He jerked his attention back to the kids. Clapping his hands once, he rubbed them together. "Okay, let's get started."

They'd just finished the repairs, and he'd already set up a painting station on half a sheet of plywood topping two appropriately spaced sawhorses when Dakota joined them. "Betty said you need help painting the chicken coop?"

"You're just in time." He shouldn't be so glad to have her company. He pointed at the staging area. "The paint needs stirring. There's a stir stick and brush next to the can."

It didn't take long, with the four of them painting, to get the chicken house done. Of course, JJ got more paint on his clothes than he did on the wood. Dakota had a streak of paint across one cheek that she'd gotten when she brushed a loose strand of hair off her face. He wanted to wipe the smear away, but kind of liked the look. War paint suited the marshal.

Certain that she put the same amount of concentration into everything she did—like their kiss—his pulse revved. A loud clang came from the house. Claude stood on the porch, ringing a metal triangular bar.

"Lunch is ready," Dakota said, laying her brush down by the paint.

"You and the boys go ahead. I'll clean up here and be there in a minute." He could use a moment to settle down. Dakota wasn't looking for a good-time guy, and he didn't want to audition for the role.

You can't have both, Leland. Either devote yourself to veterans, or chase Dakota all the way to San Francisco.

When he got to the house, the boys and Dakota were in

the middle of peanut butter and jelly sandwiches. JJ had a streak of both on one corner of his mouth. A sandwich waited on a plate at an empty seat across from the marshal, presumably his.

"Where's Claude and Betty? Did they already eat?" he asked as he sat.

"Apparently, they've decided to go to Astoria for their anniversary. They're having lunch along the way."

Beckett left his sandwich untouched and went to find the Henleys. He found Claude loading a worn suitcase in the back of his truck. Betty was already in the cab. He pulled Claude aside. "Dakota says you're going to Astoria?"

Claude edged around him so he could see his wife. "Yeah. For our sixty-fifth anniversary. We weren't planning anything, but when we were making sandwiches, it occurred to me we should take advantage of you and Dakota being here to watch the place. If that's okay with you? I should have asked first before we packed our bags, but Dakota said it would be no problem."

That was a lot of words all in a row for the old man.

"Of course, we can watch the place."

Claude clapped him on the shoulder. "Thanks, Beckett. Betty loves Astoria. We have friends there who own a bed-and-breakfast. They're saving us a room."

Claude walked to his truck and climbed behind the wheel. Dakota joined Beckett. Together, they watched the Henleys drive off.

"They've been married sixty-five years. That's a long time," he mentioned.

Dakota turned to him with a halfhearted, "Yeah, it is. But—there's Lancelot and Guinevere. They definitely didn't make it."

"So true," Beckett laughed, more than a little taken with how determined she was to stand her ground. How could she not get back in the boss's good graces? He had an uneasy feeling he was going to miss her like crazy. "Where are the boys?"

"They're playing in the back with the dogs."

Tucker was 'playing'? He had to see that. The dog was doing so much better, thanks to Dakota.

It turned out, Tucker's idea of play was to lie on his side, tail thumping the ground, while Preston and JJ ran at him and jumped, easily clearing the shepherd. Lucy danced around them at a distance, barking, no indication that she'd recently bruised her back foot.

"Let's head to the beach to fly kites." The boys would like that and it would give him thinking time to figure out what to do next.

"Okay. I'll clean up. You grab this lot and get them ready."

It didn't take long. First they drove to Stacy's house to get Preston and JJ's kites. His aunt Elizabeth wasn't home from her errands, so he texted her where they were going. Their feet hit the sand a little less than thirty minutes later, only to find a sandcastle festival underway along the long stretch of beach. He'd had trouble finding parking, finally getting a spot at a large lot along the south beach near Shipwreck Rock. Now he knew why.

"If we want to fly our kites, looks like we'll have to go to another beach," Beckett told Dakota and the boys. "Or we can check out the sandcastles."

Preston's eyes lit up. "We want to see the sandcastles, don't we, JJ?"

JJ nodded emphatically. Beckett was glad to see Preston had recovered from his earlier sadness.

"That means we'll have to put off our kite-flying date one more time. Is that okay with you?" he teased Dakota, curious which way she would jump.

She didn't disappoint. Cocking her chin, she half grinned. "I'm very disappointed but can probably wait for another day."

"Rain check?"

"Sure. Looking at sandcastles will be more fun, anyway." She winked at him and his pulse took a lethal leap.

Don't lose your head. The lady was not promising any more kisses.

And at the end of the day, she was still leaving.

With the dogs on their leashes, he ushered the boys toward the first sand sculpture, a clever depiction of a dragon lying on his back, picking his teeth with the tip of his sword.

"Wow—"

He had to grab JJ by the back of his shirt to keep the youngster from breaching the rope strung to keep the crowds back from the artists and their work. "Hold on there, buddy. You can't go past the ropes."

"Why not? I promise I won't hurt the dragon."

Squatting in front of the little guy, Lucy lying on the sand next to him, Beckett ruffled the kid's hair. "I know you wouldn't, but not everyone would be as good as you are. So we have to set an example and stay back so the artists will have plenty of room."

"Okay." JJ dropped his gaze, scuffing the bottom of his tennis shoes along the sand.

"Tell you what. How about we check out the rest of the sandcastles and then, when we've seen them all, we'll get ice cream cones?"

"Yes!" JJ said with a fist bump.

Beckett had to laugh. Ice cream always did the trick. JJ and Preston hurried to the next sculpture, which was an artistically designed hobbit house. Following closely in case he needed to remind JJ again to stay on the visitors' side of the ropes, his gaze landed on Dakota.

Sometimes, there could be too many people pressing close, but she seemed to be doing fine.

"You know, if you want to make your soap using goat milk, you could buy the milk from a local farmer. I'm sure there are a few in town who would sell to you."

Her brown eyes lit up. "Thanks for the tip. I'll check that

out."

Behind a smile, he celebrated the victory. With the boys leading the way, they circled the roped-off sections that kept milling visitors back.

He might have to let Dakota go, but not before they took in the sights, and he explored with her the possibility of becoming a partner in his newest idea.

Chapter Thirteen

EVERYONE, INCLUDING TAYLOR, talked about finding that special "one." Not that Dakota had ever believed in such a thing. Even if she did, how in the heck was she supposed to know when she met this romantic marvel? More specifically, had she already met him? Was it Beckett?

She angled toward Taylor, who'd agreed to pick her up and help her to scout out goat milk. For the first time since Beckett had paired her with Tucker, she left the shepherd home. He seemed content enough staying with Lucy. Even the dog had internal wiring that alerted him he'd found his lady.

Lady and the Tramp. There was a "couple" who'd made it, but she wasn't going to mention that to Beckett.

Dakota sighed heavily. She'd done her homework after Beckett's suggestion. Taylor was taking them to the most promising candidate.

"How did you know Gabe was the one for you?"

"I didn't at first." Taylor laughed. "We were friends, and I guess you could say he grew on me."

"That seems rather . . . risky." Dakota wasn't sure she

could let a guy grow on her, but maybe that was not as far-fetched as falling in love at first sight. That would be like throwing herself off a mile-high cliff and hoping all went well when she hit the bottom.

Seemed like if a person was going to open themselves up to being that vulnerable in the love department, either way was not a good beginning.

"Maybe, but that's how it worked for me. Why? Are you thinking of taking a chance on something more than a casual relationship?"

"No. Maybe." Dakota huffed out in exasperation, "I don't know."

"Who's the lucky guy?" Taylor parked in front of the Country Market. According to their website, they were similar to a Saturday market except all under one roof and open every day of the week. They also advertised that they had all kinds of goat products.

When Dakota didn't immediately respond, Taylor perked up, a grin spreading across her face. "It's Beckett, isn't it?"

Dakota scowled. The only example she had of love that lasted longer than a minute was Claude and Betty. And Betty wasn't at the farm at the moment, so she couldn't talk to her about how she'd made her relationship with her husband work for so many years. "How am I supposed to know? I have no experience to go by."

How pathetic was that?

"Did you get butterflies in your stomach the first time you saw Beckett at The Chowder House?" Taylor pursed her lips, clearly expecting some big emotional confession.

She was going to be disappointed. The last thing Dakota wanted was to re-examine that disastrous reunion with her sister. "No. I had other things on my mind."

"I know." Taylor grinned at Dakota's sudden discomfort. "Never mind that. You're forgiven. Do you like Beckett now?"

She could almost hear the wheels turning in her sister's mind. Dakota didn't like how transparent she'd become. It wasn't helpful that uncovering secrets was a James's pastime, like other families played board games. In any case, there was no point in denying the obvious.

"I do like him. I admire what he's doing with the dogs." And she couldn't turn off this crazy desire to spend as much time with him as she could before she left.

"Do you more than like him?" Taylor sent her a don't-bother-to-deny-it look.

"Maybe." Stomach churning, she couldn't sit still any longer. "Let's go see if the market has fresh goat's milk."

She quickly exited the truck. This was crazy. Why was she so disturbed by what amounted to a small crush?

The clerk had shown her the milk and gone on to other customers by the time Taylor caught up carrying a bag of apples. "I'm thinking we should have Camille's bridal shower this weekend."

"That's kind of soon, isn't it?" Glancing over her shoulder at her sister, Dakota grabbed two gallons of milk.

"Not really. I already emailed everyone who's invited to hold the date."

Dakota rolled her eyes. Leave it to Taylor to be one step ahead. "Grab that bowl, will you? And that spoon. And that bunch of lavender."

Taylor grabbed ingredients as Dakota named them off until her arms were full.

"So what do you think? Saturday?"

"That's as good a day as any, I guess." Dakota put her purchases behind the seat and climbed into Taylor's truck. She still wasn't sure how she'd gotten coerced into participating in hosting a bridal shower for Frank's new wife.

Maybe, Frank getting married again wasn't such a bad thing. Just because it hadn't worked out with Laney didn't mean he shouldn't find happiness if he could. No matter how much she'd wanted them back together when she was a kid, Frank and Laney were probably better apart than together. Which was exactly her point.

"Thanks for coming with me today." She stared out the side window at the passing scenery.

"I'm hoping now that you live in San Francisco we'll get to spend more time together."

Taylor was right. An eleven-hour drive once in a while was nothing if she wanted to see her family. "What time do you want me there on Saturday?"

"About nine? That will give us an hour to get things set up."

"Okay. Is there anything you want me to bring?"

A playful glint lit Taylor's blue eyes. "Actually, there is something you can do. I haven't had a chance to talk to Grant about the cake. Can you go today, pick one out, and then bring it with you on Saturday? I'll call and let him know to expect you. He owns Rose's Bakery with his grandmother."

"Taylor—"

"I know. I said I would get the cake and should have already picked it out, but it's been a little crazy at work." She turned onto the drive leading to the farmhouse.

That wasn't what she meant and by the way she tapped her fingers on the steering wheel, Taylor knew it.

Dakota raised her brows. "Angel Point is a small town. How can your work be crazy? It's not like you're chasing down drug runners." That was big sister's job.

"Not what you'd expect in a small community, right? It's just that something feels off, and I can't quite put my finger on what it is." Taylor parked but left the truck running. "Never mind. Do you need help getting all this inside?"

Beckett came around the side of the house, the dogs following at his heels. "Nope. Looks like the cavalry is here."

Taylor snickered. Dakota felt the heat rise in her cheeks. "I'll call and let you know which cake I get."

"Good." Before Beckett got close enough to hear, Taylor said, all teasing gone, "You know, you were always Frank's favorite."

"Was not." Dakota was appalled. Never once did Frank indicate that was true.

Taylor wouldn't give up. "Was, too."

Then Beckett was there, loading up with the supplies she couldn't carry because she already had her arms full.

"Hey, Taylor," he said before asking Dakota, "Where do you want these?"

"In the barn."

She frowned at her sister as she closed the truck door. Taylor smiled gently, mouthing, "It's true," before driving off.

There's no way. Taylor had to be pulling her leg. She wouldn't rib her about Frank, but Dakota couldn't think of a single reason why her sister would say such a thing.

In the barn, she put the milk in the minifridge that had been tucked behind the crates and still worked when they plugged it in. Beckett put the supplies on the shelves set up for that purpose. The barn was quiet without Betty here to show her how to proceed. The house was too, for that matter.

"Have you heard from Claude and Betty?" They were walking toward the house.

Beckett held the back door open. "Nope. I'm sure they're having a good time. They're due back on Friday."

Just in time for Camille's shower. Maybe Betty would want to go.

Beckett, the Henleys, their farm, learning to bake bread and make goat milk soap, it all had come to mean something. Dakota had walked away from so many people in her life. Could she do that again? San Francisco and Angel Point were worlds apart. She couldn't quit hers just because her girl parts, and okay, maybe her heart too, got all excited every time Beckett was near. Or was that the result of not wanting to go back to her self-imposed seclusion?

What she needed was a comparison. Her senses were so full of Beckett. She should at least take Taylor's advice and go on a date with this Grant dude.

"Want to go out to lunch?"

"Sorry, I can't. I promised Taylor I'd order the cake today."

"I have an errand too. Do you want company?"

The smile including her in his plans almost made her give in, but she shored up her defenses. Sure, in a pros-versus-cons matchup, Beckett weighed in heavily on the pro side. He was attractive, of course. That was a given. And great with kids and dogs, always a plus. She could tell he cared what happened to the Henleys. It warmed the region around her heart considerably. All good qualities in the perfect man.

Except she wasn't looking.

"That's okay. I'm not sure how long my errand will take,

but thanks for the offer." How long did it take to meet a stranger and ask him out on a date for a mid-afternoon snack? "See you later?"

"Sure."

In a hurry to get out of there before she changed her mind, Dakota patted her thigh. "I'll take Tucker with me. Come on, boy."

Rose's Bakery wasn't hard to find since it was on the next block up from Faith's Attic.

She found a spot to park out front but sat there a moment, rubbing sweaty palms on her pant legs.

This is no big deal. For Pete's sake, you chase down the bad guys for a living. Get your caboose in there and order that cake. And while you're at it, if an opening presents itself, ask the baker out on a date.

The pep talk wasn't much help, but she couldn't sit here forever.

There was no sign posted saying dogs weren't allowed, so she took Tucker in with her to bolster her courage. As soon as they entered the bakery, Dakota was assaulted by the scent of every kind of pastry and bread. The back wall was covered in brick display cases made of dark polished wood and glass. Tempting pastries filled the bottom shelves. Mouth-watering cupcakes of every variety crowded the top one. On a side wall were cookbooks. On the other, baking supplies and a sign promoting cooking classes. White tablecloths covered the few scattered tables around the periphery.

"Can I help you?" asked a white-haired woman behind the counter. She didn't appear to be as old as Betty, but she wasn't a young chick, either. Her name tag said her name was Esther.

"Hi." Dakota almost wrung her hands she was so nervous. "I'm looking for Grant Reed. I'm supposed to meet with him. The sheriff sent me."

"He's my grandson." Esther smiled kindly. "Just a minute. I'll get him for you."

Dakota waited beside one of the tables, watching as a teenage girl took over the counter and a steady stream of customers. Popular place. Except for the idea of asking a stranger out making her sweat, she may have found her second-most favorite place in town.

Talk about growing on a person. Angel Point was doing just that.

A man came toward her from a side door. He was kind of cute, but his style guru must have taken the day off. He wore a white chef's jacket, the top button left unbuttoned, allowing the flap to flop haphazardly to one side, revealing an eye-popping lime-green T-shirt underneath. Faded jeans had definitely seen better days. He wore open sandals.

Unable to tear her gaze away, she frowned at his socks, trying to figure out what was wrong with them, aside from the fact that they were the brightest color of red she'd ever seen. And then she realized what had her puzzled. One sock had blue geometric designs and the other orange and yellow interlinked circles.

Dakota arched her brows. The whole mismatched thing appealed to her funny bone, making Grant Reed not intimidating at all.

"Dakota James?" His voice was steady, appealing even. Not as deep or disturbing as Beckett's. Longish, blond hair was pulled back into a man bun. Blue eyes studied her with interest.

"Yes." She held out a hand. "I hope you don't mind that I brought my dog into the bakery."

"Not at all." He took the hand she offered. Firm grip. No sparks. Yet. "Taylor said you're looking for a cake for a bridal shower?"

Her worry dissipated. "For Saturday. Is that too soon?"

"It's doable." His smile matched the lady's at the counter earlier. Kind. Sweet-natured. Not the least bit butterfly-worthy. "What kind of cake are you looking for? Chocolate? Red velvet? Carrot?"

Dakota drew her brows together slightly. "I'm not sure. This is my first time buying a cake for a shower. What do people usually order?" Taylor could have at least given her a hint.

"First time, huh?" His smile broadened as humor launched in his eyes.

Was Grant flirting? If he was, still no nervous attraction like she had every time she got close to Beckett.

Barely preventing an eye roll, with a relieved grin, Dakota nodded. She could play this game. "I've had a lot of firsts since coming to Angel Point."

"Well, I'm glad I can be one of them." His laugh and wink were fun but didn't wobble her knees. "I'd suggest chocolate or red velvet. They're the most popular."

She was about to take his advice and order one of each until she noticed a woman with her two daughters choosing cupcakes. "What if I order a variety of cupcakes instead? I don't know, like three dozen? Is that too many?"

"It would give you and the ladies at the shower more variety. And cupcakes always go over well." He picked up a menu from the table. "Here's a list of your choices."

She took the menu but was still watching the mom with her daughters. The girls were about the same age she and Taylor were when Laney left. She had no memory of going to a pastry shop with her mother. Or with Frank after, though she was beginning to think he coped as best he could with his motherless daughters.

His daughters.

The mom paid for the cupcakes, and the little family secured one of the empty tables. She'd spent a lot of years madder than a cat stung by a yellow jacket at Frank. Maybe it was time to tell the only father she'd known that she wasn't mad anymore.

She glanced at the menu and picked out five flavors that should make Taylor happy.

"I'll deliver them Saturday morning."

"You don't have to do that. I can pick them up on my way to Taylor's."

"It's no trouble." He didn't seem to be in a hurry to get back to his kitchen, which should have stirred up some boy-girl interest on her part, shouldn't it? "Really, no trouble at all."

She took a breath. *Just do it, James.* "Can I buy you a cup of coffee?"

Grant's smile widened, if that were possible. He was awfully free with his flirting. "I'd be glad to have coffee with you. Let me tell my grandmother I'll be gone for a while."

She felt a pinch of envy, before she remembered she worked in the family business, so to speak, with Frank and Taylor.

"Okay, ready to go." Grant had left behind his chef's jacket. The lime-green T-shirt definitely said, *here I am.* He seemed so nice otherwise. A poor taste in wardrobe shouldn't be held against him.

Dakota headed for the door and the one place she knew that served excellent coffee. "How about Ginger's Coffeehouse?"

"I have a better idea. I haven't had lunch. Have you been to The Chowder House?"

That would be a big fat yes. "On the first day I came to town, I met Taylor and Gabe there." She couldn't remember what she'd eaten, but there was no need to go into her humiliating introduction to Gabe, Beckett, and the town.

"At this time of day, it won't be crowded. We can slip in and out for a bowl of the best chowder you've ever had. What do you think?"

She stopped beside her Mustang. "Should we drive?"

"This is yours?" He whistled low in appreciation. "She's a beauty and I would love a ride, but The Chowder House is just down the street, so we can walk."

That was okay with Dakota. It would give her more time to get to know Grant and see if there was any possibility of sparks. "Do you like being a baker?"

"Love it. My grandmother taught me to bake as an after-school project to keep me out of trouble." He was really quite cute when he smiled at the memory.

"And it worked?"

"Mostly." He turned slightly toward her and winked. "How about you? Do you like being a marshal?"

"How do you know?" she had to ask, even knowing the answer. She said in unison with him, "It's a small town."

Grant laughed.

Giving into the inevitable, she nodded. "I like being a marshal. You could say it's in my blood, but I actually enjoy the work too."

Angel Point was a cozy, sweet town. She could honestly say she was taken with its charm: the shops, the well-kept streets, the shopkeepers, the folks who lived here, the sound of seagulls flying overhead, the distant sound of surf rolling into shore.

But the fact was, she was proud of being part of her team too. She might have started out on the wrong foot with Granger—she could fix that. And she would, as soon as she got back.

She just had to find a way to visit as often as her work allowed, to see her family, Tucker and Lucy, and—

"I need to send a quick text." She moved out of the way of other pedestrians.

Won't be back as soon as I thought.

She got a quick response. *Everything okay?* She paused but a date wasn't a big secret, like what her next assignment was, or which bad guy she was chasing across multiple state lines at any given moment.

Going on a lunch date.

No immediate answer this time, which shouldn't have disturbed her, but did.

She resumed her stroll with Grant. They'd reached The Chowder House before Beckett texted back.

Enjoy.

Dakota frowned at the single word on her screen, because she already knew. If there was a competition between Beckett and Grant for the man most likely to make her heart thump out of her chest, the former Viper pilot would win hands down, accompanied by unforgettable Fourth of July fireworks.

Chapter Fourteen

"STAY BACK, LUCY." At the side of the house where he couldn't see the driveway, Beckett swung the ax in a high-reaching arc. The log split in two, each half falling onto the piles on either side of the stump he was using as a chopping block.

He stepped back and leaned on the handle of the ax. Lucy plopped down nearby, cocking her head as if she couldn't figure out what all the fuss was about.

Well, he couldn't either. It was late afternoon, and he had a suspicion, but it was hard to explain. He tried anyway. "She's out on a date. Probably with the guy her sister wanted to match her up with. What I can't figure out is, why do I care?"

Lucy barked in apparent sympathy. In the few days she'd been with him, she'd put on a bit of weight, filling in the hard angles that were so prominent when he'd first almost run her down. No one had come looking for her, so he figured she was part of the family.

Beckett shook his head. He was talking to the dog as if she understood. He guessed, in a way, she did, man and his best friend and all that.

At least, she was a good listener.

"You think I should ask her out on a date?" He scratched his chin. "It can't be a half-baked date like flying kites or making bread, but a serious adult date. What do you think? Where should I take her? Someplace that serves great food. The woman lives in San Francisco. For Pete's sake, she has her choice of five-star restaurants there."

He placed another chunk of wood on the chopping block and snapped his fingers. "I know just the place, but I should wait at least a day before I ask her. So she doesn't think I'm just trying to show up the other guy. Right?"

Lucy jumped up with a bark. She liked his plan. Beckett laughed at the comic picture of him pouring his heart out to the furball. Dakota had told him she was on a date. That meant, either she trusted him enough to be open with him. Or she was sending him a message: move along, mister. He would find out if it was the latter in short order. If it was, he still wanted her to know she had friends and family who cared, no matter what decisions she made.

Suddenly, Lucy took off at a dead run for the front of the house. Beckett heard the sound of a car coming up the drive and started to follow, but slowed his pace. He didn't want Dakota thinking he'd been holding his breath until she got home, even if it was true.

He cared for her. Not in a casual, he'd get over it in a week or month sort of way, either. He hated to use the "L" word, even in secret to himself, since she had such strong feelings about love being the harbinger of heartbreak. But there it was, the potential of making a colossal misstep staring him straight in the face.

He was certain Dakota was great at her job. And chances were she'd say goodbye and go.

He rounded the side of the house just as she climbed out of the Mustang, holding a paper bag close to her chest. He didn't want to scare her off, but a real date at Emilie's could be just what the heart doctor ordered. He hoped.

Unfortunately, she was as stubborn as they came, though he had to admit, he kind of liked that about Dakota. He just didn't see how a long-distance anything was the answer. She would have her job and he'd be torn between pulling together the details of the veterans' village and keeping up with her in San Francisco.

"Do you need help with anything?" he asked. *With more than carrying in groceries?*

"Thanks. That would be great." All, but whatever emotions making her brown eyes look almost black, was locked down tight. She motioned toward the back seat. "I got some things at the market to make chocolate chip cookies. And I brought chowder home for dinner."

Her date. If she was going to date anyone, Beckett was surprised at how much he wanted it to be him. Getting them there was the challenge.

"What did you do today?" she asked. "I spent the morning chopping wood."

He put the groceries on the kitchen counter next to the bag containing the chowder.

"I know nothing about shopping wood. Clearly, I make a better marshal than I do a farmhand."

"You do okay." Beckett took orange juice from the fridge and poured them both a glass. At least she wasn't shutting him out. "Do you like being a marshal?"

"I do," she conceded.

It was a silly question. Of course, she liked her work. Otherwise, she would be considering staying in Angel Point. Which made perfect sense to him. Her friends and family were here.

Polishing off his orange juice, he glanced at the clock. Nearly four. There was just enough time to stack the wood he'd cut and give Dakota some space, while he thought through what he really wanted and how far he was willing to go to get her to change her mind about having a permanent guy in her life.

"That chowder smells good. I'll finish up outside, then be right in."

The last thing he saw on his way out the back door was Dakota taking a deep breath. Had he left her a little breathless? He hoped so.

He spent the rest of the evening considering various plans to convince Dakota he was the guy she should take seriously. Through dinner and warm cookies for dessert.

During a quiet game of Scrabble he teased her into as the sun set in glorious color. A last cup of coffee on the porch in companionable silence.

Not once during the evening did she mention her date with Grant. If he was lucky, it wouldn't be repeated. He did get her to talk about her job, how much the work meant to her, some of her old cases, how she was ready to go back, and would . . . soon. Subtlety wasn't in Dakota's makeup. He got the message loud and clear. Don't get his hopes up.

At the end of the evening, he had an outline of a campaign. The dining room at Emilie's Inn was the place. He was counting on the restaurant to live up to its reputation.

Their easy conversation lasted until they went upstairs to their separate rooms. She hesitated on the landing. With the lights turned off, except for the hall light casting cozy shadows, all he wanted at that moment was to pull her close for a lingering kiss.

She smiled hesitantly. "Thanks for this evening. It was fun."

"You were fun," he said, leaning against the doorjamb as she backed into her room.

"Good night, Beckett."

No repeat kiss. That was too bad. "Good night, Dakota."

When he finally fell asleep, he dreamed of one beautiful, work-focused U.S. Marshal who was chasing felons all the way back to San Francisco.

WHEN BECKETT CAME downstairs the next morning, the only sign that Dakota was already up was half a pot of warm coffee in the coffee maker and a foil-covered plate of bacon, eggs, and toast. The rest of the kitchen was spotless. He checked out front. Her Mustang was still here. That left only one place where she might have retreated to.

He found her where he expected. Engrossed in making soap. "Good morning. How long have you been out here?"

She glanced up from adding what looked like oil to a milky mixture in a stainless-steel bowl. "About an hour. Couldn't sleep."

On a rack off to the side sat bars of the finished product. He knew nothing about making soap, but Dakota was completely immersed in her new interest.

"I'm heading into town to buy some baby chicks. Want to come along?"

"I think I'll stay here. I'm kind of in the middle of this recipe."

He stepped closer to watch as she used a long, handheld blender to carefully mix the ingredients. "I can wait."

"You should go. This is going to take a while," she half muttered.

He swallowed a chuckle, admiring her intense absorption. No point in putting her guard on notice. "Shouldn't be long. I may need your help when I get back."

"I'll be done with this batch by then."

Beckett had almost left the barn when he realized he'd forgotten something. He retraced his steps. "Thanks for breakfast. It was delicious."

This time when she looked up, she grinned. "Thought I'd surprise you with some of my cooking skills."

"Nice surprise. Knew there was a wannabe chef hiding somewhere inside that tough marshal interior," he smirked.

"Ha, ha. Go get your chicks," she ordered with mock sternness, but she was still grinning.

He almost didn't go. For a minute, he wondered if Dakota was flirting. Maybe he wasn't so far off the mark after all. "I'm going to leave the dogs here. See you later."

"Uh-huh." She was already back to the soap.

His spirits practically danced a jig while he drove to the Coastal Feed Store. The baby chicks were for Preston and JJ, but he was starting to think maybe he could get a surprise for Dakota too.

It was a long shot at best. The promise of adding goats to Leland and Company Farm would not necessarily induce Dakota to make Angel Point her home, even on a part-time basis.

It took a little longer than he planned to get the chicks and supplies. Beckett slowed as he came to the Baldwin property. He had a better view of the house. It was a ranch house, not as picturesque as the Henley farmhouse, but it had lots of potential. His attempts to get in contact with

Harry Baldwin hadn't panned out. All he'd been able to do was leave a message.

When he parked at the farmhouse, Dakota sat in one of the rockers on the porch, watching as he got out of the Bronco. Tucker and Lucy napped at her feet.

He carried the chicks to the porch. "Want to see?"

She rose from the rocker and leaned over the box containing the chicks. "Oh my! They are so cute. Can I hold one?"

"Sure." He waited until she cupped the loudest chick in both hands. "Let's take them out back to their new home."

"It's so soft." She laughed, delighted, the sound one of the sweetest things he'd ever heard.

Barely restraining from behaving like a teenager with his first crush—oh, who was he kidding; his mom would say he was smitten—he let the other five go free on the straw-covered ground in the chicken coop. They immediately started exploring and pecking. Dakota added her little chick. Beckett closed the door to keep the chicks from scampering out, but they were more interested in the container of feed he'd left before going to town.

He leaned on the corner of the coop to watch the fun little creatures. "Think Preston and JJ will like them?"

"Oh yeah. They'll love them." She squatted, poking a finger through the mesh wire. "What are we doing next?"

Leaving the chicks to make themselves at home, he pushed away from the chicken house, and headed back to the Bronco. "Claude wants the paddock on the other side of the barn repaired. He's thinking about getting a goat for Betty, since she's making soap again."

He held open the passenger-side door. "Jump in."

"Where are we going?" She gave him a quizzical look.

"It'll be easier to unload the fencing by the barn."

It took the rest of the morning and most of the afternoon to make the repairs. He still had to build an open-sided shed for protection against the weather, but that would have to be done another day. Hopefully, before Dakota had to leave.

They were in the kitchen making grilled ham and cheese sandwiches for dinner when he decided now was the time.

He fed the dogs. She plated their food. He carried them to the dining room while she brought two glasses of iced tea.

Enough already. Dakota doesn't bite.

Scrubbing sweaty palms on his pant legs, he asked, "Would you like to go with me to Emilie's Inn for dinner tomorrow night?"

She put her sandwich down. "A date?"

"A grownup date," he clarified.

Her brows came together. "Why?"

Would her suspicious nature ever be reassured? Easing back in his chair, he shrugged one shoulder. "I've never been to Emilie's. I thought it might be fun to take you and check it out." There was another reason, and beating around the bush wouldn't get him anywhere. It was time to tell the truth, or he'd regret it for a long time after she left. "And, I like you."

She stared at him, probably trying to decide if she believed him or not, but then she said quietly, "I like you too."

"So, it's a real date?" Beckett let out a huge breath. "Trust me?"

She didn't answer, but she didn't say no, either.

THE NEXT DAY, Dakota entered the barn, hoping to distract herself with a quick batch of soap, only to find she wasn't the only one who got up with the sun. Betty was inspecting the soap bars from the day before. "Morning. I heard you and Claude come in late last night. You're up early."

"This is my favorite time of day." Betty sniffed one of the bars. "You've done nice work here. Smells like you used lavender for the scent?"

"I found a bottle of lavender oil in one of the boxes. I hope it's okay that I used it. And I added fresh lavender, too, to give it texture."

"It smells lovely," Betty said with a smile.

"Did you have a good time in Astoria?"

"Yes. It's always lovely there."

"I wonder—"

"What do you wonder, dear?"

"What's your secret?"

"To what?"

"Staying married for sixty-plus years?"

Betty laughed. "There is no real secret. You just take things day by day and find ways to stay together."

"Seriously?" There had to be more.

"Seriously." Betty put the bar of soap back on the worktable. "It helps to love your guy with your whole heart, and be smart enough to know when to compromise."

Dakota started stacking the bars on the shelf. "Well, I envy you and Claude. I don't know that I could do it."

"That's because you haven't met the right man yet."

Beckett's strong face flashed before Dakota's eyes. If love were a real thing—and the jury was still out on that—it took longer than a mere fourteen days to fall in love, didn't it?

"You're a smart woman, Mrs. Henley." Dakota gave Betty a quick hug. "Would you like to go to Camille's bridal shower with me tomorrow? I shouldn't be, but I'm a little nervous about getting a new stepmother."

There, she'd said it out loud. That should count as being brave, shouldn't it?

"I haven't been to a bridal shower in years. I would love to go." Betty patted her hand. "Maybe Camille is as nervous as you are."

"Maybe." Dakota squeezed the older lady's arm. "Betty? There's one more thing." She took a deep breath and blurted it out. "I have a date with Beckett tonight, and I don't know what to wear. I didn't bring a dress with me."

Betty almost squealed, making Dakota laugh. "When did

this happen?"

"He asked me out to Emilie's yesterday, before you got home," she said, heart pounding as if saying it out loud might make it a fantasy and not the real thing.

Clearly going on a casual date with Grant had not prepared her for dinner at a fancy restaurant with Beckett. It would be fun to impress him and make his eyes pop.

Betty grabbed her hand and led them excitedly toward the house. "I've got several dresses. One of them should work."

Before Dakota knew it, she was standing in Betty's bedroom while the older woman pulled several dresses from the back of her closet.

"I'm sure these are out of style, but you might like one of them. I was a lot thinner when I bought them, so I think they'll fit." Betty laughed, clearly enjoying herself.

Vintage dresses, bright and colorful. Any one of them would impress Beckett. She crossed her fingers and settled on the emerald, classic swing-style dress that whispered around her knees when she walked. There were shoes, which miraculously fit, and jewelry to match.

With Betty's last-minute help with her hair, she was ready by the time Beckett said they would leave for the restaurant. A little breathless, she joined him in the living room, and his eyes did indeed pop.

"You look beautiful." His deep, appreciative tone made her skin tingle.

For the first time in her life that she could remember, Dakota was overcome by a wave of shyness. She lifted her chin. Be brave, she chanted in her head. She did not want to sit in the back seat, figuratively speaking, anymore.

"Thank you."

No more being afraid. If Taylor could overcome their motherless childhood and workaholic father, why couldn't she? Especially, on the arm of such a handsome, caring man.

Chapter Fifteen

IT WAS A short, nerve-racking drive to Emilie's. Beckett parked in the parking lot of a long, two-story hotel. "We're here. The restaurant is over the entry there, on the second floor."

He quickly rounded the vehicle, held the door open, and helped her out of the Bronco. With that kind of attention, how could she not be impressed herself?

Seated at a table that had a full view of the ocean and sunset, Dakota wasn't sure she'd ever seen anything as stunning as that view, unless it was the man sitting across from her, wearing a black suit that stretched perfectly across his strong shoulders.

"Nice restaurant."

"I'm glad you like it." If Beckett asked her right this second to walk off into the sunset with him, it would be hard to say no. She leaned on her elbows. "How's the property hunt going?"

"I'm trying to get in touch with the owner of the place next door to Claude and Betty's but, so far, no luck."

As their meal arrived, the sun went down on the water,

adding a certain amount of—dare she say it?—romance to the night.

She finished her crab cake and salad. "Once you get the property, how long do you think it'll be before you can open for business?"

"Right away, I hope. I'll put the word out when I'm ready to take dogs. My parents will help with that. I'm thinking of building a veterans' village for vets having a hard time leaving the military behind. That will take longer." Beckett pushed his empty plate away. "How about you? What's next? How soon are you heading back to San Francisco?"

It was time to fish or cut bait. Taylor had done it. Why couldn't she? And Beckett had proven he could be trusted. So, what was her problem?

Her problem was . . . all along she'd thought she didn't trust anyone. Frank. Laney. The world at large. The one she really couldn't trust was herself.

She'd been rolling along, maybe not living her best life, but most days doing okay. She got by. Then she'd walked in on a family falling apart and lost it. Since then it took more courage than she had in her to put one foot in front of the other.

That had to stop. Right now.

"I leave in about ten or eleven days." Dakota sat up straight. "Can I ask you a question?"

Beckett frowned. "Of course."

How could she sugar coat this? She didn't bother, but it was still hard to get the words out. Reaching halfway across the table, she asked, "What do you see when you look at me? And be honest. You won't hurt my feelings."

He took her hand as he studied her thoughtfully. "What I really think?"

"Please."

"I see a beautiful lady who is brave, and bold, and who is trying to figure out where she fits."

"I don't feel brave," Dakota said softly, a bubble of surprise swelling in her chest. He understood. "At least you know what you want. For me, it's clear as mud."

"You'll get there. It just takes time." Squeezing her hand, he stood and helped her to her feet. "How about a walk on the beach?"

"Maybe not in these shoes," she laughed. Tilting her head back, she looked directly in his eyes. What she found there took her breath away. Confidence. Trust. Belief that she could come out the other side of her personal battle a winner.

She smoothed down her dress and almost didn't find her voice. "We should probably head back. I have to be at Taylor's early tomorrow to help set up for the shower. Will you be there?"

"Noooo." He shook his head. "All the men, and boys, who can are going to the beach at Shipwreck Rock to fly kites. The ladies will join us there after the shower. Do you want me to bring your kite?"

"That would be great," she said as he held the Bronco's passenger-side door open.

Back at the farmhouse, hand on his arm, she stopped him when they reached the porch. "I want to thank you for tonight. I had a good time."

She stood on her tiptoes and placed a kiss on the corner of his mouth.

"Me too," he said in that deep, low tone that had her wishing . . . and her lips parting. Strong hands cupped her face as his lips lingered on hers, coaxing, flooding her with a warmth that took her breath away.

She'd be dreaming about this kiss, how his fingers buried themselves in her hair, being so close to touching in all the right places, long after she left. Light-headed, she still had enough focus left to wonder if her heart beating out of her chest was the same as being in love.

Slowly, each second drawn out, he let her go and backed away, desire and regret mixed equally in his storm-colored eyes. "Good night, Dakota."

"Good night, Beckett."

In her room, she carefully hung up Betty's dress. It'd been the hit of the night. Turning out the light and throwing the room into darkness, except for a hint of moonlight coming through the window, a soothing reminder of her date with Beckett, Dakota crawled into bed. The last thing she thought of as sleep overtook her, and the first thing she thought about after she woke up, was that toe-curling kiss and how she wouldn't mind a second performance.

For the first time in a long time, she was the driver of her life. She'd spent enough time letting the really good things pass her by.

THE NEXT MORNING, secretly hoping she'd *accidentally* run into Beckett, Dakota went searching for her first cup of coffee. The house was quiet. On the off chance he might turn up before she left, she took her time getting ready, but the only person waiting for her when she was set to go was her octogenarian housemate. Betty sat on the couch, dressed in a pretty rose-patterned dress. Beside her was a large box wrapped in silver paper and a wide white bow.

"Don't you look pretty?"

Hands clasped primly in her lap, Betty pinked up. "Thank you."

Dakota's lingering buzz from her date with Beckett scattered. "I didn't get Camille a shower gift."

"That's all right. I thought you might not have time, so I was hoping you won't mind . . . I put both of our names on this one." Betty handed her the present. It was heavy.

Dakota protested, "I can't let you do that."

"Of course you can," Betty said calmly.

"Really, I can find something at Faith's Attic on the way

to Taylor's."

Betty waved her objections away.

Dakota gave in. Betty's sweet aunt Bea from Mayberry exterior hid a strong-minded woman who had a way of getting what she wanted. "So, what did we give Camille and Frank?"

"It's a tea set that used to belong to my mother. I haven't used it in years, and I would rather your stepmother have it than give it to a secondhand store or strangers."

Dakota slowly led the way to the Mustang. When she was eighty-six, she hoped she had as much get up and go as Betty. "Where are the men and dogs?"

Putting the gift in the back seat, she made sure Betty had fastened her seat belt, then pointed the Mustang toward her sister's.

Betty cast Dakota a mischievous look. "Claude and Beckett left right after breakfast to pick up Preston and JJ, so Stacy and her mom could go to the shower. They took the dogs with them. How did your date go last night?"

"It was good." A slow smile built inside Dakota. It'd been very good. "Emilie's was wonderful."

She spent the ride to her sister's talking about everything but Beckett and the new feelings swirling in her chest. By the time Taylor opened the door, Dakota had only one thing on her mind. Getting through the party so she could see the man who was tempting her to rethink her plans.

Taylor waved them in, high color staining her cheeks,

eyes sparkling. Gabe leaned against the counter in the kitchen, overseeing the coffee maker.

"I brought an extra pair of hands to help." Dakota put Camille's gift on the table and made the introductions. To her sister, she whispered, "What's with the blush? Did we come at an inopportune time?"

"I was trying to convince Gabe to set a date," Taylor whispered back.

Dakota arched her brows. Her sister was smart and resourceful. She wasn't marrying Gabe blindly. "Did you get it done?"

A grin spread across Taylor's face. "September fourteenth. Save the date, Kodie."

Manly arms circled Taylor's waist. "What are you girls whispering about?"

"My sister's power of persuasion." Dakota slipped her arm through Betty's to include her new friend in the conversation.

Gabe laughed. "And she knows how to wield that power."

Dakota liked him more for the look he gave Taylor and the kiss he reverently placed on her temple. Taylor was right. A girl couldn't ask for more.

The only one she could see in that role in *her* life was Beckett.

Gabe's pager went off. "Looks like I have to go to the hospital. You girls have fun."

As he headed out the door, Dakota realized someone was missing. "Where's Frank?"

"He's pitch-hitting at The Chowder House so Camille can come."

Just as Taylor finished speaking, Camille knocked on the door.

Grant delivered the cupcakes right behind her, but didn't linger, giving Dakota a quick wave. "Gotta get back to the bakery."

Yup. Definitely just a friend.

They'd barely finished decorating when the guests started arriving. About a dozen, who all treated her as if she had lived in Angel Point most of her life and belonged. Except for possibly her boot camp sisters, Mercy and Paris, she'd never had her own gang of friends. It was an odd feeling but one that warmed her almost as much as Beckett's kiss.

When the games and opening the presents were finished, while Taylor and Betty cleaned up the living room, Camille helped Dakota load the dishwasher. "Thank you so much for the tea set. I love it."

"That was really Betty's idea," Dakota said, still a little embarrassed she hadn't gotten Camille her own present.

Grabbing a kitchen towel to wipe down the counters, Dakota vowed to find her own perfect gift for Camille and Frank. Because, it turned out, she wouldn't miss their wedding for anything, even if it meant wrangling some extra time off from Granger to make a fast in-and-out trip on their special day.

"That doesn't matter. It's a beautiful tea set. I already have a place picked out for it in my china cabinet." Camille gently took the kitchen towel, stalling Dakota's cleaning efforts. "I'm so glad you came today. I hope we can be friends."

"I'd like that, but I'm not very good at it."

"No worries. We'll figure it out." Camille wiped at the moisture glistening in her eyes, drawing Dakota into a hug. "We got a call last night. The lighthouse had a sudden cancellation on June thirtieth. So we took it. You'll still be here, won't you? We really want you to be at the wedding."

Emotion, the good kind, not the kind that put her in a tailspin, clogged her throat. "I'll be here."

Camille squeezed before letting her go. "Good. You and Taylor and I will get together to talk about the details. Right now, I have to get back to the restaurant. Your dad's a big help, but I don't want to leave him in charge too long."

Dakota laughed and without thought, snagged her soon-to-be stepmother back for another hug. "Yeah, he'll be reorganizing the staff and menu if you don't keep a close eye on him."

Taylor watched with her as Camille drove off, her car loaded with all the shower goodies. "You did good, Sis. I think you like Camille."

"I do. She's a far better woman than Frank fell for the first time." Dakota slung an arm around Taylor's waist. "I hope they're happy for a very long time."

"Me too. I think they will be." They were both silent for a moment until Taylor spun away, saying, "I've got to get ready for work."

"You're not coming to the beach?"

"Can't. Have to relieve one of my deputies. He has to make a trip to Portland to see his family today."

"Is Gabe going to make it?"

"Probably not. He'll stay at the hospital until the mama delivers."

Too bad. She was kind of hoping to show her support for her sister's engagement by making nice with the fiancé. After all her objections when she first came to Angel Point, she wanted to earn some points with Gabe.

Betty appeared at Dakota's elbow. "Would you mind dropping me off at the house before you go to the beach? I'm a little tired and thinking I'd rather read and have a nap than a walk in the sand."

"Sure." She drove Betty back to the farm and made sure she was settled on the couch with a book, and cookies and tea on the coffee table.

She took time to change into shorts and a tank top. It was ridiculous how anxious she was to see Beckett. Maybe he didn't feel the same way about her, but he had kissed her like he meant it. She drove slower. Her Mustang didn't like it— but, well, she didn't want to give the impression that she was in a hurry by sliding into home base, so to speak.

After parking as soon as she could see Shipwreck Rock, it didn't take long to find Beckett, Claude, and the boys. Not far away, Stacy and Elizabeth were seated in beach chairs under an umbrella. Tucker and Lucy were chasing waves between the kids and the ocean.

JJ saw her first and ran up, scattering sand across her feet. "Marshal Dakota. Can you help me fly my kite? I can't keep it in the air."

"Sure thing, buddy. I've never flown a kite, but I'll sure give it a try." She squatted next to the five-year-old. "What do we do first?"

"The string's all tangled," he told her as seriously as a marshal chasing down a felon. Tangling his kite string must be a common occurrence.

Out of the corner of her eye, she saw Beckett and Claude grin. Beckett's smile broadened when he caught her glance. She flushed. Heat climbed to her face. Surely, she wasn't as crazy for Beckett as Taylor was for Gabe?

No time to sort out her feelings now. JJ needed her help. After that, it would be her turn to finally get the promised kite-flying lessons from one hunky man. It was a plus in his favor that Beckett was all hot-guy muscles in his shorts and bare chest.

Claude wandered over. "Where's Betty?"

"She wanted to take a rest and read, so I took her back to the house and made sure she was all settled on the couch."

"I think I'll go check on her."

Dakota smiled at his protectiveness. She was starting to believe that sixty-plus years of marriage did that to you. "I think she wanted to have some quiet time."

JJ pulled on her shirtsleeve.

"All right then, let's see what we can do." It didn't take long to untangle the string. "What's next, chief?"

A happy grin spread across his face. "You hold it up in the air, and I'll start running."

"Okay." Laughing, she did as the kid instructed. As he took off, the kite slid smoothly into flight.

JJ ran along the edge of the waves shouting, "We did it! We did it!"

"Good job!" He was moving fast, lengthening the distance between them before Dakota realized how far ahead of her he'd gotten. Sudden unease building in her stomach, she kicked up her pace, shouting, "Slow down, JJ."

A strong gust of wind blew across the sand toward the water, taking JJ's kite, a bright blotch of green on white, with it. The string slid from his fingers. JJ jumped to try and catch it, landing with his feet in the water. "My kite! It's getting away!"

"JJ, stay on the beach. I'll get it!" Dakota shouted.

Not hearing her or too intent on retrieving his kite, he chased the dang thing farther into the water. Dakota took off at a run.

It all happened so fast. One minute he was in the water to his waist. The next a sneaker wave, buoyed by a gust of wind, arched over his head. When it smoothed out, racing for shore, JJ's head was barely above water and he was sputtering, choking on the surging water.

"JJ!" God! She hadn't been that far behind him. She heard shouts and barking behind her, felt Tucker at her side as she launched herself at the water.

She pumped harder, lifting her feet high to go farther, faster to where JJ was flapping his arms. He went under. Dakota was up to her shoulders in churning water when she saw a tiny hand break the surface. She grabbed the wrist, pulled JJ up and out of the water, and hung on tightly as she began swimming back to shore. Tucker led the way. It took forever, but Beckett was there to take JJ.

When they made it to the beach, Claude, Stacy with her arms clamped around Preston, whose face was sheet white, and Elizabeth rushed toward them.

Beckett held them all off. "Stand back for a minute. Give him room to breathe."

Dakota froze.

Beckett hung JJ over one arm, vigorously rubbing his back. For the longest minute of her life, Dakota held her breath. Her heart pounded. She started shaking. With a whoosh, sea water flew out of JJ's mouth, and he started to cough.

Beckett sat him up. His mom and grandmother rushed in, tears streaming down their faces.

Dakota plopped heavily on her backside, hanging her

head until her chin touched her chest. Her breath seesawed in and out. Tucker put his head in her lap.

"He's okay, Kodie." Strong hands pulled her into a hard chest. "He's safe."

Dakota would always remember the smell of ocean on Beckett as all the warmth she'd absorbed from him the last three weeks leached out. She'd trusted him. The one she shouldn't have trusted was Dakota James.

"He isn't safe because of me—"

"Yes, he is. You saved him."

"If it weren't for my carelessness, he wouldn't have needed saving in the first place," she said dully, lumbering clumsily to her feet. Every movement was a stiff-and-tired duplicate of the pain tearing at her heart.

She backed away from the man with whom, for a short time, she'd fooled herself into thinking she could share a future.

Not his fault she'd told herself a lie. It was hers. What was she thinking? She wasn't built for a family and keeping them safe. How could Beckett possibly love a woman who couldn't keep their children out of harm's way?

"Kodie—?"

Tears slid down her face. Tucker laid down at her feet. Unable to speak, she gave him the hand signal to stay. Desperately needing to get away, without looking back—it would completely break her if she did—she walked out of Beckett's life.

Numb, she drove to the farm. Betty was asleep on the couch, a book open and lying face down on her chest. Quiet as a ghost, Dakota went upstairs, packed her bag, and escaped the house without waking her friend. They wouldn't be friends any longer when Betty found out how horribly she'd failed JJ.

She would send Betty a letter when she got back to San Francisco. And Taylor, too, apologizing for not saying goodbye. Dakota sighed heavily. While she was at it, she might as well put Frank and Camille on her list of people who deserved an apology. She wouldn't be back for the wedding.

Dakota was stopped at the stoplight closest to The Chowder House when Frank barreled out of the restaurant, looking up and down the street. He saw her, ran into the crosswalk and stopped in front of her, feet balanced wide, fists planted on his hips.

She waved him away, but he didn't budge. The light turned green. The car behind her honked.

"Fine," she grumbled and leaned over to unlock the passenger-side door.

Frank crawled into the car, staring at her packed travel bag in the back seat. "What's going on?"

Clearly, he wasn't going to let her leave without an explanation. She found a parking space and pulled over before turning to face him. "I have to go."

"Why? Because of JJ's accident?"

"How did you know? Never mind." She told him everything, how she'd almost lost JJ on her watch.

Frank put his hands on her shoulders, but he couldn't hold her there and make everything better. "That wasn't your fault, Kodie. But I'm not going to be able to talk you out of leaving, am I?"

The lump in her throat refused to let words pass. She shook her head.

"I know you don't want it, but can I give you some fatherly advice?" He pulled her into a tight embrace over the center console and whispered close to her ear. "Don't hang on to the past too long. In the end, it will only deprive you of the happiness you deserve right now."

She pulled back out of his hug. "I'm sorry I won't be here for your wedding. Will you explain everything to Camille?"

He pressed his lips together, but got out of the car and didn't try to stop her when she edged the Mustang away from the curb. Just as she got into the flow of traffic moving south out of town, a Bronco squealed to a stop across the street.

Beckett and two sweet dog faces stared at her. He motioned for her to stay with the same hand signal she'd used with Tucker. Tears flowing unchecked, Dakota shook her head and followed the traffic heading out of town.

Chapter Sixteen

FOUR DAYS LATER, Beckett stared at the chicken house Dakota had helped him repair. He wasn't able to reciprocate by helping her mend her past. He didn't want to lose Dakota, but it was too late, wasn't it?

JJ pulled on his pant leg. "When is Marshal Dakota coming back? I didn't get a chance to say thanks for saving me."

"I don't know, buddy." He took the boy's hand and wandered into the barn where the soap-making table she'd set up was cleared of her last batch.

He'd left it as it was for a few days, hoping he could talk her into returning. Finally, when she wouldn't answer his calls or texts, he'd given up, and with Betty's help, had put everything back in their boxes.

How could he convince Dakota love was a real thing she could depend on if she wouldn't even respond to his overtures?

JJ kicked the barn floor with his foot. "Why did she leave?"

"She had to get back to work." The white lie stuck in Beckett's throat.

"But she didn't even say goodbye." The boy sounded so forlorn. Beckett knew how the kid felt.

He tucked JJ against his leg. "I know, kiddo."

A spark of anger lit up for a brief second before guttering out. He couldn't blame her for her reaction to JJ's near drowning. Beckett had been scared spitless too. But she had to know, she wasn't the only adult watching over the boys.

When he'd first come to town, a ton of that very same self-blame rode his shoulders. For crashing his Viper. For surviving Afghanistan when so many didn't. Angel Point and the family he'd made here had taught him, despite the losses, life moved on. That he could best honor those who he served with and those who'd gone on before him by making something good of his life, in his case, by paying it forward to other veterans, canine and human.

You know you'll have to fly again.

Beckett would never forget the sound of her voice, but he had to let go. He couldn't fix everything. Or everyone. Especially Dakota. That was her job. Somehow he wanted her to know he was in her corner, that she didn't have to fight her battles alone. He just didn't know how to convince her.

JJ dragged his feet. Tucker and Lucy, too. Since the accident, the dogs didn't stray far from the boys whenever they came over.

He scrubbed the top of the kid's head with his knuckles. "How about we go inside and have milk and cookies?" An idea came to him. It might not work, but was worth a try. "I'll let you use my phone to text Marshal Dakota."

"Yeah!" JJ walked fast toward the house, the dogs close behind.

It was cheating to let the five-year-old text Dakota. At this point, he would try anything to get her attention. And hopefully, in the process, stop Tucker's vigil by the front door.

After setting JJ up at the table with the promised milk and cookies, he handed the kid the phone with the open thread of texts he'd sent that Dakota had so far ignored. At least she hadn't blocked him.

"Do you know how to text?"

"I know my letters," JJ said proudly. Tongue sticking out of the corner of his mouth, he concentrated hard. "And Mom lets me text Grandma sometimes."

Sitting down with coffee and his own cookies, Beckett could feel the first genuine smile he'd had in days spreading across his face as he watched JJ. Stacy had said her youngest was a smart boy, and already learning how to spell and do simple arithmetic so he'd be ready to start kindergarten in a few months. Apparently, Grandma had been enlisted as home teacher.

"Cousin Beckett?"

"Yeah, bud?"

JJ didn't look up. "How do you spell Tucker?"

Beckett spelled the dog's name.

"And Lucy?"

"L-U-C-Y. That's a long text you're sending to Marshal Dakota."

"I'm telling her it's me. And I miss her. And Tucker and Lucy miss her too." His fingers moved slowly as he sounded out some of the longer words.

Beckett took a bite of cookie while his small cousin bit his lip. "She'll be glad to hear that."

JJ put the phone on the table and drank half his milk straight down. It was tough work spelling and texting.

"You text . . . texted her a lot. Did you tell Marshal Dakota you miss her, too?"

Oh man, he'd wanted to, but she hadn't given him a chance. Squinting one eye, Beckett said, "No."

His phone pinged a return text.

"It's her!" JJ jumped up, bringing Beckett the cell. "Read it!"

A little jealous the boy had gotten such a rapid response when he hadn't even gotten one, Beckett read, "She says, she misses you too."

JJ wasn't one to stand still for very long. He practically bounced in his excitement. "Quick. Ask her when she's coming back."

He sent the question as instructed but led with the disclosure that it was him sending the message for JJ.

And that was that.

When there was no response, he patted his little cousin

on the shoulder. "She'll come as soon as she can, kiddo."

JJ stuck out his lower lip. Beckett wanted to stick out his lip, too, but for a grown man that was a little ridiculous.

Preston came in carrying a bag of groceries. Claude and Betty, their arms full, were right behind.

Pocketing his phone, Beckett relieved Betty of her bags and followed Claude into the kitchen. "Any more in the truck?"

"This is all of them." Claude started unloading groceries into the pantry. Beckett stayed to help, hoping for a diversion from the profound disappointment that Dakota had stopped communicating as soon as she realized it was him, not JJ.

Out of the blue, Claude asked, "Have you heard from Harry yet?"

"No. I haven't been able to connect with his real estate agent and the Baldwins aren't back yet from Arizona."

"Betty and I were talking and we're wondering if you'd like to buy our farm? We'd have to sell eventually anyhow. The property is getting to be too much work." Claude paused for a protracted moment. "The thing is, if you buy the place, we would like to negotiate the price down some so Betty and I can stay here for as long as we're able."

Beckett leaned against the counter. That was a good offer. If he took Claude up on the deal, there would be no changing his mind. He'd be permanently settled in Angel Point. Dakota would be in San Francisco.

"What do you think?" Claude folded the last grocery bag and stuck it in the pantry with the rest.

Beckett took a deep breath, every moment he'd spent with Dakota over the last weeks spinning before his eyes, including when she'd left him on the street, watching her drive away and wishing with every fiber of his being that she would stay. Any future they might have was out of his hands.

"It's a deal. I'll have papers drawn up tomorrow."

"Good," Claude said, grinning.

But there was something Beckett had to do first. "Can you and Betty watch the boys and dogs for me? Stacy will pick Preston and JJ up in about an hour."

"We'll be happy to watch them, son."

Telling the kids to behave for Claude and Betty, he took off. It wasn't far to the airfield north of Angel Point where he'd heard they rented helicopters.

His nerves settled at the sound of the rotors starting up. The helicopter wasn't a military Viper, but once he was in the air, how much he loved flying came back. High up, surrounded by blue sky and the beat of the rotors, his confidence returned.

Dakota was worth every effort he had to give. He loved her. Period. Full stop. All he had to do was find a way to prove to her, love was a real thing. Something she could count on. Especially from him. If she knew what she'd left behind, maybe . . . He had a plan.

When he put the bird back on the ground, he sent a text

telling her about buying the Henley place, and Claude and Betty's decision to stay on as caretakers. He didn't expect a response but kept the message brief and conversational, as if they were in the habit of texting each other little snippets of their day.

He sent a second: "Guess where I am? Just finished flying. Thanks for reminding me not to give up on something I love."

Back at the farm, he leaned on the porch post. Betty had gone to bed, but Claude and the dogs kept him company. Man, it was too quiet without Dakota.

"I think your little Lucy might be pregnant," Claude said after taking a slug of his beer.

Beckett straightened. "What makes you think so?"

The older man chuckled. "Having many dogs over the years. Her appetite has been off the last day or two, and she's been a little sick when she eats."

"Should I take her to see the vet?"

Claude pushed the rocker into gentle motion. "I don't think so. Nature will take her course."

Beckett nodded. Even though he knew Dakota wasn't going to text or call, he checked his phone for the third time in thirty minutes.

"What are you waiting for, son? Why don't you just go get that gal and tell her you love her?"

Beckett shoved his uncooperative phone back in his pocket. Why not, indeed? And the only way to convince the stubborn woman she was the love of his life was to tell her in person.

"THANKS FOR REMINDING me not to give up on something I love."

"Claude and I have made a deal. I'm buying the farm and they will be staying for as long as they want."

"Claude says Lucy might be pregnant. Tucker and Lucy will make great parents."

Okay, that was it. Dakota started to text back and tell him to stop bothering her. Except—

Be honest now. Her thumbs hovered over the phone's keypad. He wasn't really bothering her, was he?

No. In fact, she'd started to look forward to the snippets of news he kept sending. She had never really thought of her life as particularly lonely. She knew people, had colleagues she went to lunch with or met in the bar for an occasional drink to talk work. But since coming back, all she did was think about Beckett, Tucker, Lucy, and everyone she'd left in Angel Point.

Even the town itself, with its quaint main street, so different from the Mission District where she lived, invaded her thoughts. For the first time, the Victorian house attic apartment she rented from another marshal did not hold the same appeal as it had when she'd first moved in.

Lowering herself into the overstuffed chair opposite her couch, she stared at the poster of Lucille Ball and the porcelain shepherd pup. She'd found them in the back seat when she finally made it home.

But San Francisco wasn't home, was it? On the other hand, how could she go back to Angel Point . . . and Beckett . . . without quitting the marshals? What would she do there? How would she support herself? Did it matter? Was she fooling herself, thinking that being a marshal was all that she wanted? She loved her job, but everything that mattered most to her was back in a small, Oregon coastal town.

She'd reported in the Monday after she'd gotten back to San Francisco. After a brief, sharp-eyed assessment, Granger had insisted she finish out her leave of absence. And since she was exhausted from the long drive back and majorly disappointed that she was on the run—again—she hadn't fought him.

What a wuss she was. Would the real Dakota James please show herself?

Despite all her previous objections to falling in love and casting happy-ever-after aside as a nonstarter, Beckett had managed to grow on her. Just like Taylor said. Now she understood what her sister meant.

Dakota loved Beckett. Completely. With every fiber of her being.

Scrolling through the texts that had started coming that morning, she began with the one from JJ. She was glad he was doing well and that he appeared to have no residual effects from his fight with the ocean. It still scared her, how close they'd come to losing him, but—

Granger was probably still at the office. The deputy marshal practically lived there.

She grabbed her badge and bag, dashed out the door at a near run, down the stairs, merging with the crowds on the streets—folks coming home from work or getting an early start on the night life.

Moving fast, dodging those who got in her way, she glanced down an alley and had gone a few feet beyond before the image of two kids surrounded by bigger boys intersected with her rush to talk to her boss.

She backed up. Sure enough, she hadn't been imagining the situation playing out. Two kids a little older than she and Taylor were when Laney left, faced off with three teenagers. The older of the two girls pushed the younger one behind her, the expression on her face fierce.

Dakota went straight back to another time, when it was her and Taylor against the world. Even Frank. She almost choked, but stopping her free fall down the familiar rabbit hole, found solid footing.

"Give us the necklace, brat," the older of the boys growled.

Drawing in a reviving breath, Dakota waded into the fray and found strength and trust in herself. "Okay, break it up."

The boys spun toward her.

"Go away, lady. This is none of your business," the leader of the gang snarled.

Dakota pulled her badge out of her pocket and held it up. "I think it is my business. Go home. If I find out you've messed with these kids again, you'll find yourselves doing time in juvie."

Glaring, the boys scattered.

Dakota slowly approached the kids. "You guys okay?"

The older one nodded, hanging tightly to the necklace around her neck. She tucked it beneath her shirt. Dakota got a glimpse of a stylized star.

"Can I take you home?" Dakota frowned as she knelt in front of them. The girls shouldn't be on the street without parental supervision.

The oldest pointed to a diner across the street. "Our mom works there."

"Let's go, then." Dakota shepherded them across the street at the light and watched until they entered the diner.

The older sister paused before going in, her fierceness dissolving into a brief smile. She waved.

Waving back, Dakota felt the weight of her childhood lift. She hadn't crashed and burned back in the alley. She'd stood her ground and claimed victory over her personal demons.

Her phone vibrated. Granger.

"James here."

Granger never beat around the bush. "I need you in the office as soon as you can get here."

"Yes, sir. On my way."

Hopefully, since Beckett was texting as if that was something they did every day, he didn't hold it against her that she'd left without saying goodbye. Her skin prickled at the memory of how she'd driven away. Truthfully, he could have changed her mind, which was why, aside from almost losing JJ—if she was being honest—giving him a chance to do that had scared the living daylights out of her.

Dakota entered Granger's office, a new plan beginning to form in her mind. Beckett versus the marshals? Like a flash of lightning, she knew who would win. It wasn't the marshals.

Her boss glanced up from the file he was reviewing. "Have a seat."

Maybe being put on leave hadn't been enough to salvage her reputation as a soldier who got her assignment done with little fuss, but it didn't matter. A picture came to mind of Beckett holding her hand after their date, and for the first time since she'd joined the Marines, civilian life looked promising.

"I have a new assignment for you." Granger took off his glasses and rubbed his eyes. They looked tired, his dark skin washed out from fatigue. He handed her the file. "I want you to head up a district task force in cooperation with the local authorities in the central Oregon coastal region."

That would be the sheriff of Angel Point. Dakota smiled, flipping through the file. "Drug smuggling?"

"They're using Hwy 101 north and south, rather than Interstate 5, to avoid detection." Watching her closely, Granger rocked back in his chair. "Can you handle it?"

"Yes, sir. I can." For the first time since coming back to San Francisco, Dakota felt like she could handle anything. Including saving a five-year-old boy with the help of the man she hoped wouldn't be a hard sell, after she'd abandoned him the way she had. And his dogs, too, of course. "I can leave for Angel Point tomorrow."

Opening the next file on the stack on his desk, Granger straightened his chair. "Good. I'll expect your first report by Monday."

At the door, she turned back. "Sir, are you giving me this assignment because you're friends with Frank . . . my dad?"

Granger looked up, held her gaze. "I'm giving you this assignment because you're one of the best marshals I've got, if you can get out of your head and stay focused."

"I can," she promised.

His black eyes sparkled, but as quickly returned to business. "Get out of here. And let me know what you need to set up the office in Oregon."

As he dismissed her, Dakota nodded at her boss. "Yes, sir. Thank you, sir. I appreciate your confidence in me."

With her new assignment in her back pocket, it was dark when Dakota returned to her apartment. She felt a little bit like JJ. Too antsy to settle down, she repacked her traveling bag before crawling into bed, thinking it would be a long night before dawn came and she could get on the road.

She was wrong. She slept through the night, waking in the same position as when she'd fallen asleep. Sunshine filtered through the windows. It was a sunny day in San Francisco. She wasn't going to be here to enjoy it though. Anxious—in a good way—to be on her way, she wrote a note to her landlord with the rent check for the next month and dropped it off on the way out. That should give her time to see if this new assignment was going to be temporary or last a lot longer. The bad guys weren't always cooperative when it came to shutting down their illegal activities.

By eight o'clock, Dakota was on the road. She tapped out the beat to the music from the radio on the steering wheel. If she drove straight through, she'd get to Angel Point by seven that evening. She tried to keep her speed at least close to the legal limit, but the Mustang did not want to cooperate.

Unable to hide her happiness, she'd crossed over into Oregon and was coming up on Gold Beach when she saw a familiar vehicle stopped on the side of the road, the driver changing the back tire.

Dakota parked across the highway from the broken-down Bronco. Admiring the view, she crossed the road. "Can I offer you some assistance, sir?"

Beckett stood and turned, his expression blank, except

thankfully, his light blue eyes were dancing. "Do you know how to change tires, miss?"

"Why yes, I do," Dakota said, tongue in cheek. "I've changed a tire or two in my time."

"Have you now? Well, I can use all the help I can get." Beckett stepped aside to give her access.

Tucker and Lucy barked from the back seat. Dakota took a deep breath of the sea-scented air. She was home. With her family.

With Beckett at her back, she changed the tire in record time and put the tools away, petting both dogs when they climbed over the back seat to get to her.

Beckett pushed away from the Bronco, where he'd been leaning. Closing the back hatch, he hijacked her hands. "How long can you stay?"

"At least through Dad and Camille's wedding?"

He drew her closer. "That's only three days away. Can't you stay longer?"

"Well, I did find a new bread recipe I want to try. And I don't know if you've heard but Tom Hanks and Rita Wilson have been happily married for more than thirty years." Pulling her hands free, she captured the face that made her pulse shoot to the moon. "Will it be okay if I stay long enough to change your tires for the rest of our lives? I would love to beat their record."

He leaned forward until their lips were close enough they shared the same breath. "What about your job?"

"I'm on special assignment." *In more ways than one.*

"For how long?"

"For as long as I want and you're willing."

His eyes closed as he breathed her in. "I think you're going to be here for a very long time, then."

"Beckett Leland, will you marry me?" she asked softly.

Their lips met. The hungry kiss he gave her said "yes!" in every way that promised Dakota her very own happy-ever-after. Love curled deliciously in her stomach as Tucker and Lucy barked their congratulations.

The End

If you enjoyed this book, please leave a review at your favorite online retailer! Even if it's just a sentence or two it makes all the difference.

Thanks for reading *Wanted by the Marshal* by Susan Lute!

Discover your next romance at TulePublishing.com.

TULE
PUBLISHING

If you enjoyed *Wanted by the Marshal,*
you'll love the other book in....

The Angel Point Romance series

Book 1: *The Sheriff's Baby Bargain*

Book 2: *Wanted by the Marshal*

Available now at your favorite online retailer!

About the Author

Susan is an award winning author of contemporary romance, women's fiction, and dystopian romance. Like all children of military families, she spent her childhood moving from one duty station to the next. She likes to say she is first and foremost a wife, mother, sister, daughter, friend, dreamer, and novelist. These days, when not working as a Registered Nurse, she remodels her house and writes whenever she can.

Thank you for reading

Wanted by the Marshal

If you enjoyed this book, you can find more from all our great authors at TulePublishing.com, or from your favorite online retailer.

TULE
PUBLISHING

Made in the USA
Coppell, TX
30 July 2023

19776896R00141